"You have a st on me, Coralie."

Jake pulled her close, his eyes searching as he continued. "You seem determined to needle me, but why should you? What have I ever done to you?"

Coralie realized he'd done nothing—until now. Now he was having a strange effect on her, too. His close proximity, the touch of his hand on her skin, were affecting her breathing. She tried hard to sound nonchalant. "I . . . you're talking in riddles again."

"Again. What do you mean?"

Coralie was suddenly aware of his growing anger, but unable to understand its cause.

"Let go of me, Jake. You're hurting my wrist."

"Then count yourself lucky," he warned, "because what I really want to do is put you across my knee and paddle you."

Claudia Jameson lives in Berkshire, England, with her husband and family. She is an extremely popular author in both the Harlequin Presents and Harlequin Romance series. And no wonder! Her lively dialogue and ingenious plots—with the occasional dash of suspense—make her a favorite with romance readers everywhere.

Books by Claudia Jameson

HARLEQUIN ROMANCE

HARLEQUIN PRESENTS

Don't miss any of our special offers. Write to us at the following address for information on our newest releases.

Harlequin Reader Service
901 Fuhrmann Blvd., P.O. Box 1397, Buffalo, NY 14240
Canadian address: P.O. Box 603,
Fort Erie, Ont. L2A 5X3

Unconditional Love

Claudia Jameson

Harlequin Books

TORONTO • NEW YORK • LONDON
AMSTERDAM • PARIS • SYDNEY • HAMBURG
STOCKHOLM • ATHENS • TOKYO • MILAN

Original hardcover edition published in 1988
by Mills & Boon Limited

ISBN 0-373-03001-0

Harlequin Romance first edition September 1989

CHAPTER ONE

'MISS DIXON? Coralie Dixon?'

'Yes, speaking.' Coralie did not know the voice, it was deep and gruff, not particularly pleasant and certainly not friendly. 'Who is this, please?' she asked politely, hoping against hope that it was someone who wanted a job doing. After living in Salisbury for just a few months, her funds were seriously depleted and things were not working out as well as she had hoped.

When she had said goodbye to her family in the north of England, they had told her for the hundredth time that she was mad, that she had to be to give up a well-paid, secure job. They had never got used to the idea of her leaving, even though they had known for months that she was saving up for a deposit on a place of her own. It wasn't her leaving home—she was, after all, twenty-three and perfectly capable of looking after herself—it was her leaving Yorkshire that had bothered her parents so much.

To be fair, she had sprung on them her decision to do that very abruptly, simply because it was a decision *she* had made abruptly. It was a decision she had reached in the space of one hour when she had made her escape from that dreadful scene with Malcolm Winstanley, when she had walked around in the pouring rain in a state of shock, wondering what to do. As she had walked, she had relived the awful scene over and over, resurrecting the fear she had felt—while at the same time she had been barely able to believe it had really happened, that the man had behaved the way he had.

5

But it had not been a figment of her imagination, it had been a nasty experience and it had happened, and it had jolted her, causing her to act...perhaps a little too hastily as far as her move to Salisbury was concerned. Only time would tell. Only time would tell, also, how much she had been affected emotionally by her experience on that rainy night. One change had taken place in her which actually went against her nature; basically she was a very friendly person, but she had become guarded to some extent, determined to watch herself carefully when it came to dealing with strangers—not that Malcolm Winstanley had been a stranger to her, far from it, in fact. She had told no one what had happened; instead she had decided to get away from Bradford, far enough so there was no danger of her coming face to face with him again. The next morning she had told her family that she intended to leave Yorkshire, that, as she was on the brink of moving out and changing her life-style anyway, she was going to move to a city she had always liked.

They had not understood that; they could not see why she should want to move away from the area where she had been born and brought up, where everything was familiar. And for what? they had asked. To move to Salisbury where she knew no one, where there was no work lined up for her, where she would have nothing except her 'big ideas' of making life into what she wanted it to be? What they had realised, though, was that Coralie would stand firm on her decision, which she had.

She had moved to Salisbury, she had invested all her savings in a small but perfect flat and she was happy—except for the lack of work. There were plenty of decorators around, but she was a decorator with a difference; the only trouble was that the public at large didn't *know* about her. Advertising in the local paper had been the obvious thing to do, so she had done it, but it was also expensive, and her initial splurge of quite large advertisements had yielded very little. The jobs were trickling in slowly, very slowly, and most of them were plain, straightforward decorating jobs, not at all what she really wanted to do.

'My name is Samuel,' the voice on the phone continued, 'Jake Samuel. You've been recommended to me by Mrs Garner, and I'd like to know if you're free to do a job for me.'

Coralie's eyes closed as a wave of relief washed over her; she needed this work badly and, while the name Jake Samuel meant nothing to her, she remembered the charming Mrs Garner very clearly. 'Ah, yes,' she said, 'a very nice lady.' When this was met with nothing but a grunt, she went on, 'And how can I help you, Mr Samuel?'

The reply was brusque. 'I just told you, I want—hang on a minute.'

The line clicked and Coralie was met with a sudden silence, a silence which went on for so long that she was almost tempted to hang up. The man was gone for ages, time enough for her to ponder his attitude, time enough for her to turn a few pages of her diary, pages she already knew were blank, and to wonder if he would ever come back on the line.

He did, startling her as he spoke. 'Are you still there?' He made no apology for keeping her so long. 'Right, as I said, I want you to do a job for me, but it has to be finished by Saturday evening. You do work on Saturdays?' He added this as if he needn't really have asked, implying there would be something abnormal about her if she didn't work on weekends.

'I—could, certainly.' Coralie's hesitation was deliberate. While she did urgently need funds, she was not going to let a prospective client know of her near-desperation. For one thing it might reduce the price she would get, and for another she didn't yet know what she was committing herself to. He wanted a job finished by Saturday evening—so when did he want her to start it, and, more importantly, how big was the job?

She asked both questions, but not before telling him, with her fingers crossed, that she had, as it happened, had a cancellation and was free this week.

'How very convenient,' he said, making her wonder whether he believed her or not. 'So you could start first thing in the morning?'

'I could.' There was no hesitation this time.

'OK, what I want is a mural on a wall measuring seventeen feet by ten, in my house.'

Half to herself, Coralie repeated the measurements. 'That's a fair-sized wall, Mr Samuel. Whether I could finish by Saturday depends entirely on two things: this Friday is Good Friday, how do you feel about someone working in your home then?'

'Makes no difference to me,' he snapped. 'I'll be working at home myself for the rest of the week. So what was the other thing?'

'That's a question of what you want for your mural. What exactly is it going to be?'

There was another silence, a brief one broken only by the faint sound of his breathing. 'I haven't the foggiest,' he said at length. 'Something like the effort you did at Mrs Garner's, I suppose. Hold on again, will you?'

Again he was gone, leaving Coralie with mixed reactions frowning at his reference to her artistry as an 'effort'. That she didn't care for the man's tone was neither here nor there, a client was a client, and this one was obviously a very busy person. He was probably in an office and subject to interruptions; she had heard the buzzing of an intercom before he'd disappeared this time. She was both intrigued and bemused as she waited for him to get back to her. That Jake Samuel didn't have the foggiest idea of what he wanted painted on his wall didn't fit. How could he be so positive about when he wanted her to start and when he wanted her to finish, then be unable to tell her what it was she was expected to create in the space of four days, including Saturday?

When he came back on the line, she plunged in first and tried to make sense of the situation. 'Mr Samuel, am I to take it that this mural is for a child's room?'

'Yes, my child's bedroom. Didn't I say that?'

'A boy or a girl?'

'What?'

'The child,' she said patiently, 'is it a boy or a girl?'

'Oh. A boy. A four-year-old.'

They were getting somewhere finally. A four-year-old boy would not want the Cinderella scene she had painted for Mrs Garner's little daughter. 'All right, supposing we discuss the mural when I come to give you a quote?'

'That'll have to be tonight, of course.'

Coralie clamped down on the ripple of irritation his attitude provoked. In any case he was right; if he wanted her to start work in the morning, either he or his wife had to decide exactly what was wanted, and the sooner the better. She did not bother explaining that she would have to make sketches, nor did she bother to point out the necessity of buying materials; clients often didn't think of such details, of the background work that went into a job. 'Of course,' she agreed, injecting patience into her voice again. 'So if you'll give me your address and——'

'That won't be necessary now, I know your address and I'll pick you up when I've finished at the office.'

'Well, if your wife's at home, I could drive to your house this afternoon, actually, and discuss things with her.'

In a voice which told her he was also exercising patience, he said, 'I haven't got a wife, Miss Dixon. There's me, my son and my housekeeper.' His tone hardened suddenly, so much so that she feared he was about to tell her to forget the whole thing. 'I am an extremely busy man, as you may have gathered, and frankly I fail to see why you're making an issue of things. My office is in Salisbury, in the High Street, and I have to drive past your building on my way home. I'm simply asking if I might pick you up when I've finished work, drive you out there, discuss our business, then put you in a taxi back to Salisbury.'

This time Coralie had to bite her tongue; he was talking to her now as if *she* were a four-year-old. This phone call had been all wrong from the start, but it would be stupid to allow personalities to affect her business decisions, most especially when she wanted this work not only for the money but also for the sheer pleasure of it. Jake Samuel was commissioning her to do precisely what she enjoyed most, creative work—and creating a fantasy for a child, at that. At least, she hoped he would commission her. 'As you wish,' she told him. 'You're the client, Mr Samuel. Just tell me what time I should expect you.'

'Between six and seven,' he muttered, and promptly hung up.

Coralie dropped the receiver back on to its cradle, reminding herself that it took all kinds to make a world. That was her mother's favourite saying, and how right it was! She glanced at her watch and decided to make a pot of tea. It was almost four o'clock, perhaps she would make a few sketches anyway. Since her curious client had nothing in mind for the wall of his son's bedroom, he would probably be open to suggestions—he would probably be grateful for suggestions. No, not grateful, he didn't seem the type to be grateful for anything. He had been pushy and impatient, almost rude at times, taking her totally for granted. She shrugged, heading for her tiny, compact kitchen and telling herself to put Jake Samuel out of her mind for the next couple of hours.

She succeeded in that, in fact she jumped when the doorbell rang, when a glance at her watch told her it was six forty-five. As usual she had been carried away while she'd been working, and hadn't noticed the time. Quickly she slipped into the shoes she had discarded and smoothed down the legs of her jeans as she headed for the front door, the only door, to her flat.

As she often did, she had forgotten to take off the security chain, and it was this that prevented her from swinging the door open. With a mumbled apology she pushed it closed and unlocked the chain, putting a smile on her face when she finally got the door open fully to admit her visitor. 'Sorry, I haven't been out today and I forgot to——' The words died on her lips, her eyes widening in surprise as she took in the sight of the man who was facing her.

His own eyes, seeming intensely blue in spite of the poor light in the outer hallway, were looking at her with blatant curiosity, a look of surprise equalling her own. For just a few seconds she held his gaze before dissembling, determined to keep her own impressions to herself. She had felt an element of dislike for Jake Samuel when talking to him on the phone . . . but the look of him was something no one could object to!

He was all male, broad and tall and very dark. He had been an extremely handsome man a few years ago; not that he was getting on in years now—far from it.

His age was in fact difficult to guess without close scrutiny, he could have been anywhere between thirty and forty, but the impression Coralie had was of a face that had aged before its time. There was stress in its features, marring its good looks with deep grooves between heavy black brows. She felt sure he must frown perpetually, just as he was frowning now.

'You're Coralie Dixon? You're younger than I expected.'

Her smile was determinedly friendly. 'Is that a good thing or a bad thing?'

'It's irrelevant.' He shrugged, looking over her shoulder. 'Do you live alone?'

'Yes.' She resisted the temptation to ask him the relevance of that. She stepped aside and invited him in, allowing him to precede her. 'The living-room is straight ahead.'

'I know,' he said. At least, that was what she thought he said. In the centre of the room he stopped, taking several moments to look around before nodding in approval. 'Very nice, too. You've done wonders with next to nothing.'

'I beg your pardon? Next to nothing? You mean, with such a small room?'

'That's partly what I mean.' Without waiting to be invited, he sat. 'It seems so light and airy, you've been very inventive. You'll have done your own decorating, of course, but what about those shelves and all these mirrors reflecting the light?'

Her smile was genuine now, one of pleasure and pride. 'Yes, I did the decorating, but I didn't put up the shelves and the mirrors. I'm no carpenter, I'm afraid. I had the ideas, that's all, then I paid someone to do the work.'

He spoiled everything then; she had begun to think she had misjudged him until he spoke next. 'So you're good at slapping on paint but useless with a hammer, is that it?'

Coralie was annoyed with herself for letting this go the way she did; she was unsure whether her motives were right for keeping quiet. Was she doing so because she needed the work, or because the man really did not realise what he was saying? Had he actually seen the work she had done at Mrs Garner's house or not? If he had, his reference to her 'slapping on paint' was an insult. If he hadn't, then he didn't know what he was talking about. She gave him the benefit of the doubt, merely nodding when he suggested they get a move on.

'Let's go, Miss Dixon. It's almost seven o'clock.'

'I'll just get my coat. Oh, and make it Coralie, would you? I feel old when someone keeps calling me Miss Dixon.' She flung the last words over her shoulder, wondering whether she would need a coat or just a jacket. It was early April and the fickle British weather was as unpredictable as ever. What to expect over the Easter holidays was anybody's guess; even the forecasters seemed unsure.

She went back into the living-room wearing a full-length coat and a pair of suede boots. Her would-be client was standing in the middle of the room again but this time his attention was drawn to her rather than to her décor. He was looking her over carefully, his glance taking in everything from her blonde curls to her baggy, flat-heeled boots. It made her self-conscious, feeling sure she was overdressed and...and wishing she had put high heels on. Jake Samuel's height was not extraordinary, he was six feet or six feet one, maybe, but from her point of view of five feet two he seemed menacing.

It was only with that thought that she realised what she had done: she had allowed a complete stranger into her home, she had told him she lived alone, and she was about to get into his car and drive with him to—where, exactly? Impatiently she pushed her suspicions away, acknowledging that this was all part of the change which had taken place in her since the episode with Malcolm Winstanley. By no means did she judge all men according to him, but sometimes she did feel suspicious, despite what her logic told her.

Her logic? Since when had she relied on that? As she glanced at Jake Samuel again, she knew without doubt that she had nothing to fear from him. It was not logic but intuition which told her that—and her intuition had always been reliable. His attitude might be unpleasant, but there was nothing actually menacing about him. Still, there was something...something other than his attitude...making her feel uncomfortable. Maybe it was the intense darkness of those frowning brows, that untamed hair, jet-black with a mass of curls even more unruly than her own. Or perhaps it was the unmistakable physical power of the man. Beneath the immaculate cut of his jacket, the muscularity of his back and shoulders was evident with even his slightest movement—and he was moving towards her, his hand going firmly beneath her elbow as he steered her towards the front door.

Pointedly she moved away from his grasp. 'I do know my way out, Mr Samuel. I've lived here since Christmas and I think I can remember where my front door is.'

That he was obviously taken aback gratified her. His black brows lifted slowly, as if she had challenged him. 'I see no need for sarcasm, Coralie.'

'Then why do you persist with it?' She could have bitten off her tongue at once. Oh, how many times in her life had she blurted like that, unable to resist saying precisely what she was thinking? And she had done so well until now: she had reminded herself that tact was not her strong point, so she should watch it; she had even kept in mind that he was not the first difficult client she'd had, nor would he be the last. So why had she spoken out like that?

Because it was her nature, that was why, and her innate bluntness would not be suppressed. At least, it wouldn't with this person; with this man particularly she had held back until she could hold back no longer—but he provoked her, whether he knew it or not.

'Perhaps you'll explain that remark—that question?' This was all he said; they were outside in the hall and he was still walking, with a stride it was difficult to keep up with.

Cursing herself, Coralie took a few seconds to think. Her flat was on the second floor, but Mr Samuel was not bothering with the lift, he turned towards the staircase, giving the impression that he knew the building and its layout perfectly. Well, at least they were still heading for his car, which meant she hadn't been fired before she had started!

'It was your remark about my slapping on paint,' she explained. 'I resented it.'

'I see.'

'And I didn't like my meticulous work at Mrs Garner's being referred to as an "effort", either.'

'I see.'

They were parallel with one another on the stairs, and she glanced at him quickly. It told her nothing, his face was impassive except for the frown; that was still firmly in place, but then it always had been. 'I spent four years training as an artist, Mr Samuel. I do decorate rooms— I mean I do hang paper and I do paint walls plainly, but I do that simply because I have mortgage repayments to make. When I'm established, when all my capabilities are known, I shall do what I really want to do all the time.'

'I see,' he said again. Then, with only the mildest interest, he turned to look at her briefly. 'And that is?'

'Painting murals, making mobiles, painting pictures——'

'As in pictures for hanging?'

'As in pictures for hanging.' She paused, trying to hold back the question she wanted to ask. It was more than she could resist. 'Did you see for yourself what I did at Mrs Garner's?'

'No, actually I didn't. I took her enthusiasm, her recommendation, on trust.'

'So, from your own point of view, you're really dealing with an unknown quantity.'

They had reached the main door of the building and he stopped, turning to look at her closely now. 'So it would seem, Coralie. So it would seem.'

That, it appeared, was the end of their conversation. When they got outside there was a slight drizzle falling, but it was not cold. Silently, Jake Samuel pointed across the forecourt, his finger indicating a sleek black Jaguar which, it seemed to Coralie, suited him admirably. She slid into the passenger seat, tucking in the folds of her coat before he closed the door and walked around to the driver's side. Still nothing was said.

They buckled up and drove off in a silence that lasted and lasted, every minute of which made her feel more uncomfortable. To guess what was going through his mind would be an impossibility, so she didn't even try. Nor did she regret what she'd accused him of, although she might have if he had not taken it so well.

Or had he? Again she glanced at him, this time surreptitiously, as he drove, his attention fixed on the traffic in the darkening night. Privately she admired the way he handled the big vehicle, steering it easily, assuredly, on the slick roads as they weaved their way out of Salisbury. It occurred to her that she had not asked him how far away he lived. She should have: petrol expenses had to be taken into account when she quoted a price for a job.

Without realising it she sighed audibly, wondering if this new life of hers had been a mistake, after all. Maybe she should have stayed in Yorkshire, near her family if not actually living with them, safe in a permanent job which had at least produced a regular salary, if little satisfaction. She had wanted so much to do her own thing, to earn not a fortune but just a comfortable living from work which gave her pleasure. And the result so far? She was having to count every penny she spent. Was she doing something wrong, somehow, or was she merely being impatient, expecting too much to happen too quickly? Whatever, she was not defeated yet. Wasn't she on her way right now to quote for a new commission?

A sudden belt of rain against the windscreen brought her head up. It was then that the silence inside the car was broken. 'I was wondering where you'd gone, Coralie. You've been staring at your hands for the past ten minutes.'

'I was thinking. I was—er—I was wondering where you live, exactly.'

'We're almost there, just a few miles. I live in Grovely Wood, if that means anything to you.'

'Not really, I'm not that familiar with the area. I'm from Yorkshire.'

'So I hear.'

'From Mrs Garner?'

'From your accent.'

'Oh.' She turned to look out of the window, not that she could see much. Buildings were getting fewer and farther between, and she had no doubt the scenery was lovely in daylight.

Again nothing else was said until Mr Samuel drew the car to a halt outside a large, sprawling bungalow which immediately captured her imagination. The outside lights were such that she could make out a lot of detail, she couldn't discern the actual colour of the building but she could see the exterior was wood, that it was dark and, though it was a modern-looking building, it was by no means incongruous in its setting against masses of trees.

It was, in fact, a gorgeous home. They entered through a huge kitchen, which her client referred to as 'the back way', moving through that to a spacious dining-room, elegantly furnished, with expensive rugs on a parquet floor. Beyond that was a wide, wood-panelled corridor leading to other rooms, one of which was the living-room. Coralie glanced in as they passed its open door, noting the plush, deep purple carpeting and the fact that the room was on two levels. It was, she assumed, L-shaped, since there were two steps disappearing round a corner on the far side.

'Mr Samuel?' Again she wasn't thinking, she was just talking, being herself. 'Is that your living-room? May I see it?'

He stopped, turning to face her with a shrug. 'If you wish.' With a wave of his arms he gestured for her to go ahead. Coralie stepped into the room, while behind her he flicked on the lights.

She realised her mistake at once, sucking in her breath at the sheer size of the room, it was even bigger than she had thought, and the carpet was not deep purple but deep red. She took it all in at once, the lines of the furnishings, which were a little tired-looking but still luxurious, the lighting which accentuated the alcoves filled with books, others housing glasses and decanters. She took in the paintings and wished she had more time to study them, at the same time thinking how she would just love to get her hands on a room this size, with such potential. She did all of this before turning to look at the man standing behind her, unaware that she had been surveying the place for minutes rather than seconds, unaware also that her face was alight with enthusiasm, her sea-green eyes brilliant with it. 'I love it!' she said, her arms moving out in a wide circle. 'I just love it. You had to be joking when you admired my place!'

For seconds he said nothing, he merely looked at her before asking, 'Joking? Or was I being sarcastic?'

She might have expected that; she supposed she deserved it. 'No, you weren't being sarcastic on that occasion.'

'How can you be so sure?'

Coralie was still smiling. 'Because when you're being sarcastic, something about your voice changes. It didn't when you complimented me on my living-room.'

He smiled then. It should have been no big deal, but it was, because his smile changed his face completely, chasing away the frown and revealing white, even teeth. Even his eyes took on a different hue; she could see now that they were every bit as blue as she had thought them, intensely blue. But his smile vanished as quickly as it had appeared, he was looking beyond her at the room now, and suddenly the frown came back. 'This room needs redoing from top to bottom. It's getting shabby.'

'No, not shabby, it's just lived-in ... as a living-room should be.' Her attempt at lightness failed, he was determined not to see her little joke, not to stand around talking any longer. He told her curtly that he wanted to get on with their business—while Coralie had to remind herself that that should be her own attitude.

'Stuart's bedroom is this way.' He flicked off the lights and stepped back into the hall, leaving her to trail behind him.

Again he flicked switches, throwing light into every corner of his son's bedroom, which Coralie thought was a strange thing to do. The child had obviously been settled for the night and would surely wake up now. She was wrong about that. The bed was empty. 'Oh! I thought—your son isn't at home, then?'

'Evidently.' He sighed, held up a hand, unsmiling. 'All right, all right, I'll rephrase that. No, Stuart is not at home, he's with my sister in Fordingbridge, and tomorrow he's going into hospital there for a few days. Until Sunday.'

Coralie's delicate eyebrows shot up. 'Nothing serious, I hope?'

'Nothing serious. Tonsils, that's all. Hence my surprise.'

'What? I'm sorry——'

'My surprise. When I bring him home on Sunday morning, he's going to find your mural on this wall, isn't he?'

'Indeed he is.' She looked at the wall he was pointing at. The bottom three feet of it was covered entirely by built-in units, bookcases and shelves, mostly filled with toys. This meant she would be working almost entirely from a step-ladder.

She stood, surveying the job, enjoying the host of ideas tumbling through her mind, ideas which presented themselves as pictures already painted on the wall, one after the other. Since this was going to be a surprise for Stuart, he obviously hadn't expressed his own preferences for the decoration. 'And you have nothing particular in mind?' she asked the boy's father, finishing her thought aloud. She didn't turn to look at him, she was aware he had moved away from her but she was preoccupied, getting the feel of the room and its contents.

'How about Superman with a billowing cape? Or Spiderman or Action Man—or all three?'

Dismayed, she let her eyes close, blotting out the pictures when she realised that her ideas and his were miles apart. 'Not for this child, surely?'

'Well, what else would a four-year-old boy want?'

Her eyes came open; she was at a loss to understand the man. He should know the answer to that even better than she; the only experience she had with children were those she met in the course of her work, and they were talking about *his son*. And one thing was for sure, this four-year-old was not ready for Superman or any other 'man' of that ilk. The books on the shelves told her that much, as did the toys. There were umpteen teddy bears around, tatty and well loved teddy bears, and about the same number of furry rabbits. *All* the toys were of a gentle nature. She ran her eyes carefully along the contents of the shelves, knowing exactly what this child would like. 'Mr Samuel, how many teddy bears did Stuart take with him to your sister's house?'

When he didn't answer she turned to look at him. 'I said—— ' She stopped short, wanting to laugh, but finding herself unable to. Jake Samuel was sitting in a very small armchair which his big body overflowed to a ridiculous extent, making her wonder how on earth he had squeezed himself into it at all. Her amusement never surfaced, though, because he had shifted his eyes to the floor and the expression on his face was an unreadable one; she knew only that it was far from being happy. 'I—don't know,' he said at length. 'He took a box of stuff with him.'

Something was wrong here, she knew it and he knew she did. So how was she going to ask him whether his son was a normal four-year-old? How did one put such a question? Happily, she didn't need to.

'Stuart's a boy just like any other boy,' she was told. 'If you don't like my ideas, then use your own.'

'I—well, I was thinking about Paddington Bear or Peter Rabbit or Rupert, perhaps?'

'Rupert?'

'Rupert *Bear*, Mr Samuel.' She gestured towards Stuart's toys, wondering why the man couldn't see what was under his nose. 'Your son is obviously crazy about rabbits and bears.'

'Oh. Yes, I suppose he is.' He pushed himself to his feet, leaving the inadequate armchair rocking with relief. 'That's it, then. Stick them all up, all three of them and any others you care to think of.'

And that was that, apparently. He was standing by the door, holding it open. Coralie shook her head helplessly. 'If you don't mind, I'd like to stay in here and think for a few minutes. You go ahead, by all means.'

He did, and, when she joined him in the kitchen five minutes later, the kettle was just boiling. Further along the work-surface, there was what looked like a defrosted, home-made meal.

'I've phoned for a taxi,' he informed her. 'It won't be long. Will you have a cup of coffee before you go?' The question came almost reluctantly, adding to Coralie's impression that he couldn't get her out of his house quickly enough.

It was because of that that she declined the cup of coffee she was actually gasping for. Not knowing what else to do, she sat at the kitchen table to wait for the taxi. Only then did she register how very quiet the house was. 'Your housekeeper doesn't live in?'

'She lives in a small cottage at the back of my property. But she's away this week, on holiday. She took the opportunity while Stuart's not here.'

'And your wife? I take it——'

'You can take it that my wife is dead, Miss Dixon. I'm not divorced, I'm a widower.'

In the awkward silence that ensued, Coralie fished into her shoulder-bag for a tissue, just for something to do. Jake Samuel was looking at her with open dislike as he moved towards the table, a steaming mug in his hands.

'I'm sorry,' she said softly. 'I didn't meant to pry.'

'You weren't.' He wasn't looking at her any longer, he was raking his fingers through his hair, seeming exhausted and tense. Not knowing how else to fill the silence, she quoted him for the mural.

It got a reaction. He looked at her in astonishment and laughed, actually laughed. 'You must be joking!'

Panic gripped her. 'Mr Samuel, there's no way I can do it for less.'

'For *less*? You're crazy, you're underquoting by miles! You have all your materials to buy, you have running costs for shunting back and forth, your work for four solid days, all this plus the hours of preparation—assuming you work from sketches—and for a pittance? Why should you do that? If you're as good as you seem to think you are, why undersell yourself? What sort of businesswoman are you, anyway?'

Coralie blinked at his outburst, thinking it was the most he had ever said to her in one go. What could she say in reply? 'I—I'm beginning to wonder...'

'Then wonder—you do just that—because I'm going to accept your quote—and let it be a lesson to you.'

'But——'

'There are no buts. I shall pay you not a penny more than you have asked for. I will, however, give you the bonus of some advice. I can put a lot of work your way, which I will if I'm satisfied by what I see, but your coming cheap is not an answer to your problem. Undercharging for your talents can rebound, you know. It's bad psychology, for one thing. If you're really good, I mean. You say you're trying to get established in Salisbury—but as what? Think about it, think how many people *won't* hire you because you're so cheap.'

'And if I'm cheap, I can't be any good?'

'Exactly.' With that, hearing before she did the sound of a car pulling up, he got to his feet. 'Your taxi's here. And, Coralie, you may add the cost of it to your bill.'

Half stunned by all this, feeling grateful for it and slightly resentful all at the same time, she quipped, 'I'll do that, and I'll include the tip!'

Jake Samuel had no sense of humour, none at all. He didn't laugh, he looked heavenward. 'Don't be a smart Alec. You can take my advice or you can leave it, that's up to you. You can carry on thinking it's all a big joke, too, if you prefer. It's no skin off my nose.'

'But I wasn't, I mean——' She never got to say what she meant, never got to thank him. He had opened the door to the taxi driver and he kept his back to her, being very obvious in his wish to get rid of her.

CHAPTER TWO

IT WAS just after nine when Coralie rolled up at the bungalow the following morning, itching to get her hands on that big wall. She had spent several hours doing new sketches the night before, poring over the host of books she kept for reference, and at the crack of dawn this morning she had breakfasted, showered and dressed early so she could get to her supplier's as soon as they opened. She was all business today, which was as it should be, and, no matter what her client's attitude might be, her own would be strictly professional, friendly but detached.

She climbed out of her old but thus far reliable van, and glanced admiringly at Jake Samuel's home in the morning light. Beautiful—it was bigger than she had realised, low and long and elegant, fitting its surroundings inconspicuously. She envied him living in a place surrounded by trees.

Intense, unsmiling man that he was, as she waited for him to answer the door she wondered again what sort of mood he would be in and what he did for a living. He had told her he would be working at home today, and she wondered how it was that he worked both at an office and at home, and how he could put some work in her direction. She had been so taken aback by his 'advice' the previous evening, she had neglected to ask him.

Jake Samuel didn't answer the door. Instead, he spoke from directly behind Coralie and she spun round, jumping at the deep tones of his voice. He had come out through the open garage, and without a 'good morning' or 'how are you?' was asking if he could help her inside with her things.

'No, thank you. I can manage.' She moved away to open the back doors of her van, aware again of her smallness when he looked down at her. For practical reasons she was wearing flat shoes today, and denim dungarees under which there was a cotton blouse. Her hair was in the ponytail she always wore when she was working, the top of which was covered, together with the soft curls of her fringe, by a headscarf.

'That's a...different sort of outfit, Coralie.' She heard the words as he followed her to the back of the van, but she said nothing, she jumped into the vehicle and started lifting out tins of paint, declining his help again when he offered to carry her step-ladders.

'Those things are almost as big as you are—or should I say as small? Let me carry them for you.'

Coralie jumped back on to the driveway and glanced up at him. He was looking her over and his amusement, though suppressed, was unmistakable. 'Mr Samuel, please don't think——'

'Jake, make it Jake.'

'Jake, please don't think that because I'm petite I'm also helpless. I've been shunting ladders around for many years now and I haven't dropped a pair yet, nor have I strained myself. Excuse me.' She disappeared into the van again, hoping he had taken the hint and gone.

He hadn't, he was leaning against the outside of the vehicle, his hands in the pockets of his slacks, watching her lift the ladders to the floor. 'How come?'

'How come what?'

'How come you've been shunting ladders around for years? You told me you'd trained as an artist.'

'I often helped my father at weekends, since I was about twelve, actually.'

'He's a decorator?'

'He is.'

'A decorator with a difference, like you?'

'No, a straightforward, good old-fashioned tradesman who paints insides and outsides of houses and offices and factories.'

'I see. I'd wondered where you learned the decorating side of things—and I'm wondering now why your father never taught you to cost a job properly.'

Again he was standing in her way, making her walk round him as she piled things on to the drive. It occurred to her that he was doing it on purpose, but she dismissed the idea as too ridiculous. 'Would you excuse me, please? I want to close these doors and you're in the way.'

He moved, still surveying her with amusement. 'A professional female decorator is an uncommon acquaintance in my book, except for interior decorators, that is. I know several of those. Come to think of it, I can't say I've ever run across a woman who does the actual labouring before.'

He was doing it again, standing right in front of the ladders. She reached for two tins of paint instead and moved towards the house, going in through the garage. She thought she would emerge in the kitchen, but instead she found herself in a recreation room in which there was a full-sized snooker table and a bar, together with several leather armchairs and standard lamps. This was strictly Jake's room by the look of it, masculine in feeling, but unused, too. Everything looked brand new.

When he spoke from immediately behind her she jumped, unaware he had followed her. 'What you're looking at now is my private space.'

She glanced over her shoulder, knowing a flash of annoyance when she saw he was carrying the ladders. She said nothing about it, however. 'Then how come it's unused?'

He ignored the question. 'Turn left out of here—you can remember where Stuart's bedroom is?'

He had cleared the room for her, having moved the bed out of the way and taken everything off the built-in shelves. He put the ladders against the wall, seeming annoyed for some reason. 'I'll leave you to it,' he said, 'unless you want help carrying the rest of your things?'

Coralie met his eyes directly, wanting to smooth things over. She had no idea how she had annoyed him, but she didn't want to work in a bad atmosphere. She gave him her friendliest smile. 'I suggest we make an agreement, Jake. We've both got work to do, so if you don't get under my feet, I won't get under yours.'

It had quite the wrong effect. Despite her smile, her friendly tones, he looked further annoyed. 'I can assure you that you'll see nothing of me at all. Since you insist on being independent, I'll leave you to lug the rest of your stuff yourself.' He did, he vanished into another part of the house and Coralie saw nothing of him until lunch time. She had stopped to make herself a cup of coffee at eleven, which she took back to Stuart's bedroom, and heard not a sound until one o'clock, when there was a knock at the door.

'I'd like to know what plans you have for lunch.' Jake stood in the doorway, his eyes on her hand as she continued painting. 'I forgot to take food out of the freezer. I thought you might like to come out for a pub lunch with me?'

'Thanks, but I rarely eat lunch. I have a good breakfast and a good dinner, but I don't usually bother during the day.' She turned to look at him, smiling, gesturing towards the wall with her left hand. 'I'd prefer to carry on.'

It seemed she couldn't say anything right. Jake's frown deepened. 'What is it with you?' he demanded. 'Do I have to watch every syllable I utter?' He retreated, closing the door very noisily behind him, leaving Coralie with her mouth hanging open, wondering what on earth all that had been about. What had she said now?

Dismayed, she turned her attention back to the wall and tried very hard to put that little scenario out of her mind. She couldn't, she was cross and she continued to be cross. What was the matter with the man? What had she said to upset him? She went over their exchange several times, and could find nothing untoward in her remarks.

When she emerged for a cup of tea and a break around four o'clock, she found Jake sitting at the kitchen table, elbows down, his head resting on his hands. The atmosphere between them at once made itself felt, hanging in the air like a cloud.

'There's some coffee in the percolator,' he told her.

'Thanks. I thought I'd have tea, actually.'

'Well, you would, wouldn't you?' he snapped.

She turned, responding with an annoyance that matched his. 'What do you mean by that?'

'I mean, you would; you'll do anything to be contrary.'

Coralie threw up her hands, she was unhappy as it was because her work was not going as well as it should—thanks to him—and if things continued like this she might make a hash of it. 'Look, this might strike you as odd, if not *contrary*, but your attitude is affecting my work and——'

'*My* attitude?'

'Yes, your attitude. And there's really no need for it, you know. I don't know what I've done to offend you. Probably nothing, come to think of it, because you were stroppy and difficult before we even met, or should I say clashed?'

He didn't answer, he didn't move a muscle for several seconds, he just stared at her as if she was out of her mind. Then he picked up his coffee-mug and walked away.

Coralie picked up the kettle and filled it, glancing over her shoulder for fear he would come back and blast her, because that was what he had seemed likely to do. It occurred to her that she could quit the job right now; she might need money but she did not need aggravation. It was only the thought of his putting more work her way that made her stay in the house. She needed all the contacts and all the recommendations she could get, and it looked as if the grapevine was going to be more valuable to her than advertising.

It was six o'clock when Jake knocked on Stuart's door again. Coralie turned, unaware of the time and curious as to his interruption. 'You needn't knock,' she said laughingly, 'this is your house, remember?'

'I knock because I don't want to startle you,' he explained stiffly. 'Because you're working on ladders, and the last thing I need in my house is a woman with two broken legs. Now, since you're obviously unaware of it, time's marching on. I'm going to the hospital to see Stuart shortly—so what time do you intend to finish?'

'Right now, if you like.'

'It isn't a question of that, that's entirely up to you. All I want to know is whether you'll be here when I get back? If not, I'll give you a key for tomorrow.'

'You're not working at home tomorrow?'

'I'm working on site.'

'On site? What is it you do, exactly?'

'I'm an architect.'

'Really?' Coralie was impressed. Thank goodness she had not allowed her temperament to make her walk off the job earlier! An architect was a very good contact indeed. She sat on the top step of the ladder, pulling the scarf from her hair. 'Did you design this bungalow, by any chance?'

'Yes. And your home, too, as a matter of fact.'

So that was why he knew his way around the building! He had designed the place. Then she realised . . . he was not Jake but Jacob Samuel. His offices were in the High Street, he had mentioned that, but she hadn't put two and two together and she must have walked past his brass name-plate a hundred times. 'So you are Jacob Samuel . . .'

'At your service.' There was no smile. He dug into his pocket and pulled out a key. 'This is the key to the back door. I may or may not see you tomorrow evening, that will depend on how late you work. Still, I've no doubt you'd prefer it if our paths didn't cross.'

'Oh, I wouldn't say that!' Coralie laughed, easing her way down the ladders to take the key from him. She looked at him with a mild sense of shock when he caught hold of her wrist. He pulled her close, his deep blue eyes searching the depths of hers. 'You are having a very strange effect on me, Coralie Dixon, and I'm damned if I can say why. I feel you're determined to needle me, yet I know that can't really be the case. After all, why should you? What have I ever done to you?'

He had done nothing—well, very little, until then. But right now he was having a strange effect on her, too, and it was something more than the irritation he was provoking in her. The close proximity of him, the touch of his hand on her skin, was affecting her breathing. Perhaps if she were really honest she would admit to feeling alarmed, regardless of what her intuition dictated. After all, Jake Samuel was a very powerful man and, just as she was to him, he was an unknown quantity. She slid her eyes from the raw penetration of his and tried hard to be nonchalant. 'I—you're talking in riddles again.'

'Again? What does that mean? What does any of that mean?' Closer, he pulled her just a little closer, but she could feel the warmth of his breath against her cheek now. She was aware of his growing anger, but she was unable to understand it, unable to understand the man at all.

'Let go of me, Jake. You're hurting my wrist.'

'Then count yourself lucky,' he warned her, 'because what I really want is to put you across my knee and paddle you.'

Later, much later, Coralie would wonder why she reacted with such violence, but that was how she did react, because his words shocked her. She forgot her alarm, she wrenched away from him and stood erect, all five feet two of her, her arms splaying out expressively, her eyes spitting fire as she let rip. 'What the devil is the matter with you? I have never met anyone so quick-tempered, so *grim*. I have never met anyone so down-right unfriendly, downright *impossible*, in my entire life! *You* don't have to watch every word you say, *I* do. And I've had enough of it. You have the audacity to call me contrary while you—you are nothing less than perverse!'

Laughter was the last thing she expected. Quite suddenly something seemed to snap inside him, as it had with her, but his reaction was to laugh so hard that his eyes became moist.

Infuriated beyond reason, Coralie spun round in search of something to throw at him. She couldn't see much, just a rag she had soaked in white spirit. She hurled the wet missile at him without a thought to the possible consequences, and when he laughed even harder she walked out. Just like that. The keys to her van were in her pocket and off she went. She slammed the bedroom door behind her and yelled through it. 'I shall collect my things in the morning, Mr Samuel. When you get back, you'll find your key on the kitchen table.'

She drove straight home, trying and failing to calm herself. She didn't care about anything just then, the lost job or possible recommendations or anything else. All she wanted was to soak her aching limbs in a hot bath; she had done too much in one day. All in all, the entire episode with Jake had been too much. *He* was too much.

She eased her van between the tools of her trade in her garage, and hurried inside to her flat. The phone started ringing as soon as she opened the door, and she snatched it up quickly before it switched on to her answering machine. Breathlessly, she snapped out her name.

'I'm not too clear about your intentions,' a voice said. It was Jake Samuel and he was evidently still amused, his voice was drenched with it. 'Does this mean you've walked out on the job?'

'You're too right, it does.'

'And what will that do to your reputation—if I gossip about your unreliability?'

'I haven't the faintest idea, nor do I care.'

'But what about your mortgage repayments? I mean, this could be the ruin of you, Coralie. If you will persist——'

'Listen,' she cut in, closing her eyes, for his merriment was barely concealed at all now. 'There are things more important than money——'

'Like what? Temperament? Foolish pride?'

She ignored that. 'If you are typical of the clients I can expect to encounter in the south of England, then I see I made a very serious mistake in leaving Yorkshire.'

'Aha!' he went on, amusing himself further. 'So it's them and us now, is it? The north versus the south. Why, Coralie, you surprise me! Don't you know the reputation Yorkshire folk have for being blunt and outspoken?'

'Certainly I know it. And you can't take it, can you? You prefer talking in riddles and indulging in moods which I can't understand.' With that she hung up; she had blotted her copybook irrevocably anyway. So that was that.

Except that it wasn't. Hours later, at five minutes to ten, the doorbell rang and Coralie put down her book, assuming automatically that it was Sophie, a neighbour she had befriended and gone out with a few times.

The last thing she expected was a visit from Jake Samuel—but there he was, still seeming vaguely amused, and looking more handsome because there was no frown between his brows.

Coralie leaned heavily against the door, searching for inspiration. She hadn't the faintest idea what to say to him. 'What do you want?'

'I want you to finish the job you agreed to do.'

She began to close the door, calmly but determinedly. 'I'm sorry, that's out of the question.'

With infuriating ease he stopped the door from closing; he simply put a hand against it and pushed it, and her, backwards into the tiny hall. 'Now, don't be unreasonable,' he coaxed. 'I mean, you can't leave me with just one single bunny rabbit on my wall!'

The words, the way he said them, made her need to laugh irrepressible; it just burst out of her even as she shook her head. 'I can. I can and I will.'

'But, Coralie, listen.' He almost crooned the words, at the same time closing the door. He moved as he talked, effectively backing her into the living-room. 'Think of Stuart, of how disappointed he'll be. The child will be coming out of hospital and——'

'I have thought of Stuart, and it doesn't wash. Since he doesn't know his room's being decorated, he can't be in for a disappointment.'

It was no use; when he pursed his lips and put a finger to them, tapping them, looking helpless and telling her he hadn't thought of that, Coralie started laughing again.

'I thought you had no sense of humour...'

'Then it just goes to show,' he said, smiling now. 'Well?'

'All right, I'll be back on the job in the morning.'

'That's a promise?'

'That's a promise. I'll make an early start.' She assumed he would go then, but no, instead he shrugged out of his jacket and flung it over a chair before making himself comfortable on her two-seater settee. 'Then let's sort out our differences and make life easier for the next few days.' He didn't wait for her comments, he just went on, 'For starters, you are far too temperamental for your own good. Artistic temperament is one thing, yours is quite another.' He paused, waiting for her to respond this time. She didn't because he was accurate, he was right; she merely inclined her head in acknowledgement. 'Ah! So you can take criticism.'

'When it's fair, yes.'

'You mean, when you agree with it,' he grinned. 'Now, would you explain how you reached the conclusion that I was difficult and unfriendly? This, when I offered to help you this morning, when I offered to feed you at lunch time.'

'I——' He had put her on the spot. She knew her summing up of him was accurate, but she did not know how to answer this question without sounding churlish. It was difficult to explain. 'It's just your attitude. I told you. I feel you've got me in your house under sufferance.'

'And I feel like an intruder in my own home. You told me to keep out of your way—and I don't call *that* friendly.'

Silence reigned for a moment, for as long as it took Coralie to make a decision. Should she tell him? Should she explain herself further? She decided against it, merely looking at him as he was looking at her, him shrugging, her sighing.

'Maybe there is a difference between northerners and southerners, after all,' he said. 'Speaking of which, where is this northern hospitality one hears about? Why haven't you offered me some coffee—or is there something stronger knocking around?'

'I'm afraid there isn't.' She hesitated, wanting him to go really, but not daring to give any hint of it. She did not dislike this man, not any longer, but she knew the two of them could never get on, even if she wanted that; they were just too different. While she acknowledged that she had over-reacted to him this evening, that in fact she appreciated his straight talk just now in trying to sort out their misunderstandings, she felt they had no more to say to one another.

'Well, Coralie? Why are you standing there looking as if you're in pain?'

'I'll put the kettle on.' She escaped quickly so he wouldn't see her smiling at his gross exaggeration.

It was only when she got in the kitchen that she remembered her state of dress. Anxiously she looked down at herself to see if anything was visible through her long nightie and gown. Nothing was, both garments were too practical to be see-through, although the look Jake gave her when she went back into the living-room could have made her believe otherwise. She became uncomfortable with him again.

There was no frown, but there was no more amusement, either, and his eyes moved over her as slowly and carefully as they had that morning, if not more so. 'This is quite a contrast. This morning you looked like a tomboy, and tonight you look—well, good enough to cuddle at any rate.'

'How kind.' She tried to be flippant, but it didn't quite come off. To her chagrin she could feel herself blushing— which was enough for Jake to start laughing again. It was a different kind of laugh, though, one which was accompanied by a long and searching look into her eyes.

'I'll say this for you, Coralie, you're different. It's a long time since I saw a woman blush like that, and with so little provocation.'

She said nothing, she couldn't think of anything to say. Silently she handed him his coffee, which she knew he took black and sugarless, then she sat carefully in the armchair she had been in earlier. Her gown stayed securely closed against the movement, but her hands went unconsciously, nevertheless, to tighten the belt at her waist.

'Relax.' Jake was watching her every moment, apparently. 'You're as safe as houses, I assure you. Mind you, I must confess that the temptation to kiss you this evening was very strong.' He was still watching her, waiting for a reaction.

She didn't make one, nor did she meet his eyes. The idea of being kissed by him was not an unattractive one, but she wasn't going to let him know it; not that he was serious, in any case.

'In fact,' he went on, 'if you hadn't been hysterical, I might have given in to it.'

'Hysterical?' She flashed an indignant look at him—only to find he was grinning. So he had been joking, and she had risen beautifully to his bait! The only way to get over the moment was to concede defeat. Softly she laughed, shaking her head and telling him she had never met anyone quite like him.

'No one quite as perverse, you mean?'

She laughed louder. 'Right. And grizzly and moody.'

'Thank you very much.'

'Your coffee-cup's empty,' she added mischievously, 'so why don't you go now?'

'Are you trying to tell me something, Coralie?' He smiled, it was an appreciative smile, and once again his eyes slid over her in a very male surveillance.

That tipped the balance for Coralie; she changed her mind and decided she would explain a few things, after all. 'As a matter of fact, there is something I want to tell you,' she began firmly, only to find herself suddenly tongue-tied. 'I—had an experience a few months ago. I mean—it happened before I left home and…what I mean is, I don't wish to get involved with any of my clients.'

'Involved?' Jake frowned, causing her to blush again because she knew he had misunderstood. 'Who said anything about——'

'I know, I didn't mean that the way it sounded. Well, yes, actually I did.'

The frown was replaced by a grin. 'I can't say you're making much sense. What exactly was this experience?'

Coralie let her eyes close for a moment, wondering how she could tell him without going into too much detail. It had been so bizarre, really, because Malcolm Winstanley was someone she had known all her life—sort of. Quite simply he was the man in the corner shop, the grocer's at the end of the street, someone who had always been there, standing behind the counter, for as long as she could remember. He had always been Mr Winstanley to her... the small, slight, pleasant man who served her when she popped into his shop now and then.

Aged around fifty, and a confirmed bachelor, he lived with his old mother who had been bed-ridden for the past six years, and, if Coralie had thought about Mr Winstanley at all when she was not actually facing him, it was with a sense of pity for the difficulty of his circumstances. Single-handedly he looked after his mother and his shop, keeping the place meticulously clean and trying to compete with supermarket prices, working very hard and earning, no doubt, no more than a reasonable living for him and his old mum.

'The details don't matter,' she said to Jake. 'What matters is what it taught me. Put it this way, if I seemed unfriendly today, I'm sorry, because in reality I'm not an unfriendly person. But I do try to keep a distance where my clients are concerned, and with all people who——'

'Who are male,' he finished for her. 'I begin to understand. One of your clients made a pass at you—right? An unwelcome pass.'

She almost laughed; he was accurate, but his guess did not go far enough. With an embarrassment she had no reason to feel, she told him there was more to it than that.

He stared at her, reacting with surprising vehemence. 'You're not telling me you were *raped*?'

'No.' Coralie smiled, knowing it could not have come to that, just as Mr Winstanley must have known it at the time. She had not been alone in his house with him, his mother had been upstairs and the walls of the house were thin enough for Coralie's yelling to be heard by the old lady. 'It was more than a pass, but it fell far short of rape.'

'But you were attacked?'

'I—yes, I suppose that's an accurate description.' It was, although it seemed too strong a word, looking back. Her fear and fury had been short-lived, dissolving firstly into disgust and then, as she had been able to look back more detachedly, into sadness. She had ended up feeling sorry for Malcolm Winstanley, rightly or wrongly. Perhaps she was too soft, but there was no escaping the thought that her own behaviour could have been partly responsible. She said as much to Jake, looking helplessly at him. 'I was far too friendly towards the man, I suppose.'

'And he was a client?'

'Sort of—I knew him, anyway. I was still employed full-time, but I helped my father out now and then, on occasional weekends and evenings. Dad was scheduled to do the work for this man, a simple emulsion job in a kitchen and living-room, but I did it because Dad got 'flu and was in no fit state.' Her voice trailed off and she glanced away, recalling the scene with very little emotion now.

She had worked in the grocer's back rooms for four evenings in total; after hours, when he had been there to chat to. He had made her sandwiches and fetched her cakes and pots of tea. That was what she was doing when he suddenly lunged at her—drinking tea . . . The job was just finished and she sat next to him on the couch, thinking nothing of it, laughing, telling him about something one of the girls had said at work that day, when suddenly he made a grab for her. In that first moment she thought he was joking. She squealed in protest, mainly because her tea slopped over the side of the mug, but it got serious very rapidly when his mouth clamped over hers in the most repugnant of kisses.

She fought him off, shouting her protest now, asking him what the hell he thought he was doing. His answer was beyond belief: he told her he had fallen in love with her. Whether he saw the stunned expression on her face, Coralie had no way of knowing, because no sooner had he spoken than he was kissing her again . . . but this time he was pinning her arms to her sides and his force was incredible. He had that amazing, sinewy strength that some small men have in abundance, and when he forced her backwards, supine on the couch, there was little she could do except yell and kick at him. It didn't stop him, and when his hand slid under her jumper to grab at her breast, she got very frightened indeed.

Looking back from the standpoint of today, now, she nearly laughed when she remembered how she had addressed him. She had still called him Mr Winstanley!

'Let go of me! Mr Winstanley, let go of me. You're hurting me—for heaven's sake, have you lost your mind?'

'Yes!' he told her. 'Over you, Coralie. You're so beautiful, so very pretty . . . I've admired you for years, don't you know that? I've watched you grow up to be the most gorgeous creature, inside and out, the kindest girl in the world. Kiss me, be kind to me, you're always kind to me. Be kind to me now, Coralie!'

She was crying by then, scared out of her wits. His hand was pulling at her bra and it snapped, exposing her breasts to his painfully grabbing fingers. At that point she screamed at the top of her lungs, bringing her knee up, but unfortunately missing her target. And all the time he was trying to persuade her to be kind to him, to love him, as he put it. It was not Coralie who brought him to his senses, it was the sudden banging on the ceiling, the forceful voice making itself heard from upstairs.

'Malcolm? Malcolm! What are you doing down there?'

He froze, staring at Coralie and blinking rapidly. Then he recoiled, pulling well away from her but still staring at her, as if she were an apparition, a dream, as if he couldn't understand why she was there in his living-room. 'Coralie? What——'

She never heard the rest of the question, she was fumbling her way blindly to her feet, frantically pulling her clothing in place. Yes, it had been bizarre, that was the right word for it. She heard his 'Coralie, wait a minute!' as she grabbed at the door-handle, immediately followed by more thumping and demands from above.

Had Coralie not somehow found herself looking at the man as she turned to flee, her subsequent actions might have been very different indeed; she might have headed straight for the police station. There again, she might not. It was academic now. But she did find herself looking at him, just fleetingly, and the expression on his face was one she would never forget. It was a look of pure terror. Not only that, he was pleading with her to forgive him, not to tell anyone, he was saying again and again that he didn't know what had come over him, that he loved her and would never, ever harm her.

The very last thing she heard as she bolted through the shop to the outer door was his pathetic explanation to his mother, shouted to her from the living-room. 'I'm coming up, Mother. It was the television, that's all, I turned it on too loudly...'

'Coralie?' Jake's voice brought her back to the present and she started, not knowing what was the last thing she had said to him. 'You were saying you'd been too friendly towards him.'

'Yes, I——' She broke off, sighing. 'And yet I was only being myself, really. Anyway,' she shrugged, 'the result is——'

'The result is that it's turned you off men.'

She laughed, shaking her head adamantly. 'No, absolutely not! I dealt with it in my own way and I have not become paranoid or neurotic or anything like that.'

'You reported it to the police?'

'No. I mean I dealt with it in my own way emotionally.' At his querying look she added, 'I had my reasons for not reporting him, Jake. It wasn't necessary. I mean, I didn't actually get hurt or—anything. The man was someone I'd known for years, a lonely, pathetic middle-aged bachelor who imagined himself to be in love with me. He was in business locally, in a very small way, and if I'd reported it to the police it would have destroyed him. I didn't tell my parents, either, because it would have amounted to the same thing. My father would have thrashed the daylights out of him.'

'So who was he?' Jake persisted. 'Tell me more about it.'

'No, it doesn't matter, it's all water under the bridge. All I really wanted to tell you was that it's made me cautious with people.'

'You mean male people.'

'Of course I do. Especially unknown males whose houses I'm working in with them—alone.'

'That's fair enough.' He nodded. 'I can understand that. I had wondered about you, as a matter of fact.'

'In what way?'

'I'd wondered whether you'd left someone with a broken heart in Yorkshire.'

'No, nothing like that. Not in the way you mean, at any rate.'

'So why did you leave, why did you move so far away? Because of this man?'

'Yes and no. I was leaving home anyway. I wanted to better my life-style, and it was high time I left the nest. I was brought up with three younger brothers, and the bigger they got, the more overcrowded our house got. I like Salisbury very much. I like working for myself and I like living alone.'

'You don't get lonely?'

'Sometimes,' she admitted. 'Just now and then. And what about you, do you get lonely?'

Tension gripped her; she had managed to say something wrong again and Jake's reaction was a sudden tightening of his mouth. It was odd the way she reacted to his displeasure, the way she attached importance to that moment—the way she decided *not* to apologise for what he clearly considered her tactlessness. 'I'm not going to apologise, Jake. If you can ask that question of me, why can't I ask it of you?'

'You can. You did.' He relaxed visibly, looking at her with renewed curiosity. 'And the answer is yes, sometimes I feel as lonely as hell.' He paused before adding, 'And of course you shouldn't apologise for being yourself, not ever.' None the less, he got up to leave.

'So I'm not forgiven?' she challenged.

'There's nothing to forgive.'

'Then why are you leaving?'

He slipped into his jacket, not looking at her. 'Because you want to make an early start in the morning and it's getting late.'

She nodded, pushing herself to her feet. 'I haven't asked you, how was your son tonight?'

'Very dopey from the anaesthetic, but fine, thanks.' He moved towards the door; she followed to let him out and put the chain on.

'Good. Well, I may or may not see you tomorrow, then.'

For several seconds their eyes met and held, seconds during which Coralie began to take seriously the remark he had made about being tempted to kiss her. She had thought he'd been joking, but she wasn't at all sure now. His eyes were moving searchingly, gently, over her face, lingering on her mouth.

'Goodnight, little fire-cracker,' he said softly, tapping her lightly on the nose with a forefinger.

Bemused, she leaned against the door when he'd gone. Fire-cracker? Well, that was how she must have seemed when she had exploded this evening, and there really had been no need for her to react so violently, not with him. She was aware of her shortcomings... but what of Jake? She had thought him a strange man in more ways than one; she had had to revise her opinion of him, yet she could not really say what her new opinion was.

CHAPTER THREE

THURSDAY morning dawned bright and sunny; the sky was an azure blue as Coralie drove to the bungalow. It was seven-thirty when she let herself in, and she had no idea whether Jake had left for the day or not; the garage door was closed and there was no sign of life anywhere.

It was typical, she thought, that of all the free days she'd had of late, this one had to be so perfect just because she would be indoors all day. Spring had sprung at last and, if she were honest, she didn't feel like working today.

She stopped dead when she walked into the kitchen. Jake was standing by the sink with a bath towel slung around his neck. He was wearing a pair of white swimming trunks and was as good as naked as far as Coralie was concerned. She stared at him in astonishment. 'You—have a swimming pool in the house?'

'Yes. Help yourself if you feel like taking a break today. It's at the end of the bedroom wing. There's a sauna, too, if that holds any appeal for you.'

'I—haven't got a swimming costume.' Nor did she know where to look; Jake's body was magnificent and the temptation just to stand there and take in the lines of it was enormous. Even as she dropped her eyes she could still see him in her imagination, solid and muscular with not an ounce of excess weight. The mat of hair on his chest was as intensely black as she might have expected, had she ever thought about it, tapering down his flat stomach to disappear mysteriously in a line beneath the trunks encasing his narrow hips.

46

'Coralie?' There was amusement in his voice. 'I said, you'll find several bathing costumes in the changing-room; they're there specifically for guests.'

'Yes, I—thank you.'

'On the other hand, why bother with a costume? You'll be here alone all day.'

She glanced at him, relieved to find he had busied himself making coffee and had his back to her. God, he was beautiful! The artist in her could hardly let that go unappreciated, and the woman in her could not deny it no matter what she thought of the man at a personal level. 'I'd better get on, Jake.'

He turned, seeming surprised. 'Coffee's on, won't you have a cup first?'

'No, thanks. I planned to make an early start and...there's a lot to do.' She excused herself and headed quickly for Stuart's bedroom, relieved to be away from the scrutiny of those deep blue eyes. He knew, he *knew* she had reacted to the sight of his near-nakedness, and that annoyed her. It was herself she was annoyed with; why did she have to be so gauche? Why had she blushed again? In a twenty-three-year-old woman it was just too ridiculous—it was just that it had been such an unexpected sight!

She set about her work by surveying what she had done yesterday and referring to her sketches. She was mixing paint when Jake came in—fully dressed in a tan-coloured cashmere sweater and trousers—but she was not aware of his presence until he spoke. She was humming to herself, crouched on her knees on the floor in the middle of the old work-sheets she'd put down to protect the carpet.

'I have to say I prefer those jeans to yesterday's dungarees, Coralie. Mind you, if they were any tighter you wouldn't be able to bend in them at all, would you?'

Coralie's head whipped round and she toppled backwards on to her behind. 'You startled me! You might've knocked.'

One black eyebrow went up, he shook his head as if he despaired of her. 'Aren't you the person who told me not to bother——'

'Yes, yes. All right. Sorry.' She waved a hand in the air and got on with what she was doing. 'I'm about to make a start,' she said, for the sake of having something to say. 'If I can get half of it finished by this evening, I'll be right on schedule.' She was feeling self-conscious again, knowing his eyes were surveying her figure in the hip-hugging jeans. Unfortunately she found Jake Samuel a little too attractive at a physical level; it was off-putting and disturbing. 'Did you want something?'

'Just to let you know that I'm leaving now. Bring a change of clothing with you tomorrow, I'll take you out to dinner when you've finished.'

This was the last thing she expected, the very last, in fact she wasn't sure he was serious. She turned to look at him to see what sort of expression he was wearing—it was an impassive one. 'Dinner?' she said, looking blank. 'Didn't I make myself clear enough last night, Jake? I thought I'd explained——'

'You explained yourself very well,' he cut in, 'and I appreciated your telling me all that. But don't compare me or confuse me with someone else, Coralie. I am not a potential attacker.'

She wanted to laugh; comparing Jake with Malcolm Winstanley was something she could never do. Hardly! Even so, she shook her head. 'I don't think our having dinner together is a good idea, Jake, thanks all the same.'

'Now what's that supposed to mean? You have other plans?'

'No.' Tomorrow was Good Friday and she had no plans. She'd had ideas about going home for the weekend, until this job had turned up, but she was actually as free as a bird. 'No other plans. I've told you how I feel—I don't think it's a good idea to mix business and pleasure.'

'I agree with you.' He was leaning against the doorjamb, an air of boredom about him which communicated irritation. 'But this is business.'

'It is? How?'

'Your business. I want to talk to you about it.'

She didn't know what to say, she was not even sure she believed him.

'My God!' he said vehemently. 'If you could see the look of suspicion on your face, you'd laugh your head off. Now, listen to me, watch my mouth and try to understand, because there is nothing complicated about this: I'm inviting you out for the purpose of talking about you and your new-fledged business, all right? There's no more to it than that, so take that look off your face and give me an answer because I have to leave now, right now.'

'Oh. Then yes, OK. It sounds—good,' she added lamely.

Jake walked away, he must have been half-way down the hall when he called back to her. 'That's another thing I've learned about you, Miss Coralie Dixon; you're about as gracious as you are tactful!'

The sound of a door closing coincided with the sound of frustration she made. So she had seemed ungracious and tactless? Well, it was too bad. He would have to add those to his list of complaints about her. She climbed up her ladders and started work on Paddington Bear.

By noon her back was aching and she knew she must take a break. If she didn't, her work would suffer for it. It was not ideal, she concluded, having to create to a deadline. Then she remembered there was a pool in the house and, the more she thought about it, the more irresistible the idea became. But why resist, anyway? She went in search of it, turning left out of Stuart's bedroom. The room next door was a bathroom and beyond that there were two guest bedrooms and another bathroom.

She opened a door at the end of the corridor to find herself in an empty space, six foot by six, off which two further doors opened. The first was the master bedroom and it was gorgeous, or rather, it had been—could be. Like the living-room, it had about it an air of tiredness, as if its occupant were turning a blind eye to its need for attention. The white shag-pile carpet needed cleaning, the curtains needed replacing. With a mild sense of guilt Coralie looked around carefully; everything was neat and tidy, the bed had been made meticulously, but this only added to her curiosity about Jake. He was a successful architect with a prestigious company of his own and he could not be short of money. So why neglect a lovely home which he had designed specifically for himself? This bungalow had to be his ideal, he was the potter of the clay and he simply must have designed his home with love and a sense of excitement. Yet the place was...somehow flat. Or was she being fanciful? Did it lack vitality, atmosphere, because Stuart and the house-keeper weren't present?

On the far wall were two more doors, and Coralie opened them without a twinge of conscience—curiosity had replaced her feeling of guilt. One door led to a dressing-room through which was a vast, walk-in wardrobe, the other room was an en-suite bathroom in which, again, everything was kept tidily. It was almost as big as her living-room, she noted with amusement.

Only then did it strike her that nowhere, not in any of the rooms she had seen, was there a photograph of Jake's wife. She thought back to the evening when she had weighed up everything in Stuart's room, but no, it was the same story there, too. There were no photographs of the late Mrs Samuel anywhere.

The pool room was fabulous; there was little in it to show signs of neglect, the tiling was immaculate and the carpet in good condition. Over in one corner was a built-in bar—unstocked, she noted, except for a solitary bottle of mineral water and one glass. There were several plants in tubs, several lounging chairs and, to the left, sliding glass doors leading on to a patio made private by the trees on the edge of the garden, where the woods began.

Coralie did not stop there. After her swim she went in search of Jake's study. She found it via the living-room, up the two steps which turned a corner. The extent of the bungalow, the clever design of it, surprised her. The thought, the ingenuity that had gone into its design was a revelation about Jake himself—and so was his study. In here there was life, a different atmosphere altogether. She stared around, looking at the drawing-board and all the tools of his profession, the books, the leather armchair he must use when he took a break. In here there were french windows leading to a patio raised from the ground. On it was a solitary garden chair and a small, weatherproof table. Was that where he sat and thought? she wondered. The setting was perfect, what with the trees, the lawn leading up to them, the silence...

Again she looked around for photographs. There were none, none at all. It struck her as decidedly odd.

Her afternoon was spent thinking about Jake as she worked. In his absence she worked well, easily, her brushes flying across the wall as they always did when she was in such a good mood. The promise of a fine day had been a false one; by early afternoon it had started raining and it was still raining now. In any case, all thoughts of being outdoors had long since gone. Come to think of it, she had thought of nothing other than Jake since the moment he had left this morning, which raised another question: had he really asked her out to talk business or was he interested in her? What business did they have to talk about, actually? And if he did show an interest in her personally—what would she do? Oh, certainly he was attractive, she appreciated that as much as the next woman would, but did she want to risk any involvement with someone who could steer much-needed work in her direction—or *not*, as he chose? No, it would be more sensible to keep their relationship, their acquaintanceship, strictly neutral. In any case, he was not her type.

'By the way,' Jake said the following evening, 'we're in for a bit of a drive tonight. Finding a decent table in a decent restaurant on Good Friday evening proved to be something of a problem.'

He was about to leave for the hospital in Fordingbridge, and Coralie was just putting her brushes to soak when he came in to see her. He was already dressed for their evening out, looking immaculate and strikingly attractive in a charcoal-grey suit, white shirt and a dark red tie.

They had arranged that Coralie would bathe and dress while Jake went to see his son; her change of clothes was hanging in a guest bedroom. It was on the tip of her tongue to say he needn't have put himself out, that they could have taken a rain-check on their dinner-date. She thought better of it, however, determined to maintain the peaceful atmosphere that had reigned all day. Jake, too, had been working for the past nine hours, but she had shared two coffee-breaks with him and had accepted his invitation to swim again at lunch time. Had he been going to join her in the water, she might not have, but he'd said there was something he had to finish and had gone back to his study.

'Well,' she said now, 'it was very sweet of you to go to such trouble to book a table.'

There was a wicked glint in his eyes when he answered that. 'Why, Coralie, what is this? Charm, for a change? Are you out to disillusion me now? Am I to discover you're not really as aloof as you appear?'

She gave him her brightest smile. 'Don't start, Jake. You've managed to behave like a nice human being all day.'

'Touché,' he said, and left.

Aloof? All the time she was soaking in the bath, Coralie thought about that. Was that how she appeared? What *did* he think of her, in fact? Not much, she was sure of it; he really didn't understand her at all, the image he seemed to have of her was nothing like the reality. Was it? Or was this a case of that old saying about every person being three different people—the person one thinks one is, the person other people see and the person one actually is?

Moreover, did it matter? She considered that and decided it did. The sensible thing would be to get on with Jake if she could, and, with a little effort, she could. Of course she could, all she had to do was let him get to know her a bit. So why was she feeling tense in spite of her blissful soak in hot water?

It didn't make her any easier when her hair misbehaved abominably. She had remembered to bring her hair-dryer but not her shampoo, and the one she'd found in the guest bathroom had done weird things to her curls. They were difficult enough to manage as it was and, the more she attacked them with the hair-dryer, the wilder they were getting. 'To hell with it,' she said at length, knowing from experience there was nothing for it but to let them do their own thing. She made up her face carefully in an effort to counter the disappointment of her hair, then she slipped into fresh underwear and an almost new, pale pink jersey dress which could be glamourised by the addition of the right jewellery.

She was in the living-room when Jake got home, having helped herself to a drink. 'I took the liberty,' she said as he appeared in the doorway, waving her glass at him. 'I thought a swift gin and tonic wouldn't go amiss.'

He seemed pleased. 'Good for you. Stand up, Coralie.'

She stood, thinking he wanted to leave immediately. She was wrong, he wanted to look her over.

'So you have got legs!' he mused, coming further into the room. 'And may I say how fabulous they are, at that?'

She looked at him uncertainly and sat down again. No, he wasn't joking this time, either, he seemed delighted by her appearance. He moved over to where the drinks were and offered her a refill, helping himself to one. Coralie asked for a tonic without the gin, knowing she had better pace herself or risk talking too much— which she did whenever she had a drink too many.

'How was Stuart tonight?' She was looking at Jake's back, admiring the cut of his suit, the crisp whiteness of his collar and the way the curls at the back of his black hair tapered into very tiny ones at the hairline.

'Well, he's enjoying all the ice-cream they're giving him, and he informed me that he might not come home on Sunday. It seems the ice-cream one gets in hospital is better than one can get at home.'

'Could be that it's more plentiful, in the circumstances.'

Jake smiled, sitting opposite her and stretching his long legs before him. 'Could well be that. I dare say he'll play on his sore throat to avoid all the green vegetables Mrs Everly insists he eats.'

'Your housekeeper?'

He nodded, drank his drink straight off and pushed the fingers of one hand through his hair. He was tired, she observed; he'd had a long day, a drive to the hospital, and now there was another drive ahead of him. The observation did nothing for her self-confidence, so she suggested that perhaps he was in no mood to go out, after all.

'Quite the opposite,' he said. 'I'm looking forward to it.' He got to his feet and proffered his hand. 'Come on, if anyone's physically tired, it's you. Do you always work such long hours?'

'That's a funny question, coming from you. You do far more than your fair share.'

'Supposing you just answer the question?'

'OK. No, I don't, only when I'm working to a deadline.' The imp in her made her add, 'For a difficult client.'

'That's my girl!' Jake threw back his head and laughed appreciatively, tucking her arm under his. He helped her into her coat and gently lifted her hair out from under it. When it was down, her hair ended several inches below her shoulders. She kept it long, layered, and he remarked on it.

'This is an evening for firsts—it's the first time I've seen you out of trousers and the first time I've seen your hair down. It's beautiful, Coralie. Naturally blonde, too, isn't it?'

And his fingers were in it. She turned to face him, effectively removing them, protesting that of *course* it was natural!

'So there's nothing false about you, eh?' He smiled down at her, but from less distance than usual; she was wearing high heels tonight.

She lifted her chin, an exaggerated look of indignation on her face. 'I certainly hope not.'

'Glad you managed to get that paint spot off your nose,' he mumbled before steering her towards the front door.

It took almost an hour to get to the restaurant, a one-time manor house in a delightful countryside setting. The path from the car park was lit with old-fashioned streetlights, the soft lights from inside the building making it look homely as they approached. It was something of a deception; the place was certainly welcoming in every way—the decor, the smiling staff—but it also had that subdued atmosphere which spelled *expensive*. Pre-dinner drinks were served in a drawing-room filled with antique furniture, wafts of sophisticated perfumes, cigar smoke and the hushed conversations of about a dozen people.

The head waiter greeted Jake by name, shaking his hand and saying how nice it was to see him again.

'It's a while since I've been here,' he said to Coralie afterwards, 'but I used to come regularly.'

With whom? she wondered. His wife? How long ago was that? He had never volunteered anything about his wife, about when she had died, or from what. Nor had she any idea what his marriage had been like, had meant to him, not that this was the time to ask such questions. She doubted she would ever ask.

Her pre-dinner drink, the second of the evening, was perhaps a mistake. She could feel the effect of it already, thanks to her empty stomach. When a huge, leather-bound menu was handed to her, she hit panic stations. There were no prices on it, on her copy at least, and it was all in French with no translations. Jake, who couldn't have been more at home in this place, asked her what she fancied. She decided honesty was the best policy.

'Well, I can translate about three of the dishes, but not the sauces, and after that I'm lost.'

He did not laugh at her; he was only too pleased to help. He moved from a winged armchair to the chesterfield on which she was sitting, and went through the menu item by item. Concentration was made difficult for Coralie; Jake was leaning close enough for her to be aware of the sharp masculine tang of his aftershave. She was torn between the necessity of watching where he was pointing on the menu and her desire to look at him. He really was a very attractive man, the planes of his face were so clearly defined, the features regular without being impossibly perfect. His mouth was nothing short of sensual, why hadn't she noticed that before? Or had she? Often her eyes were drawn to it, and his voice fascinated her, too; it was cultured, refined, but also gruff and very deep...

'Coralie?' He turned suddenly, catching her scrutiny, looking straight into her eyes. A quick smile flashed across his mouth and he asked, gently, if she would like him to order for her.

'After all your trouble?' She returned his smile, thanking heaven she was not blushing again. 'Yes, please.' She was, she realised, out of her depth, not just with the surroundings, but also with him. Jake was far, far more sophisticated than she, an experienced man to whom this sort of evening was old hat.

Having had that thought, though, she forgot about it in the ensuing hours. Not for one moment did Jake's attention stray from her. He was in every way the perfect host, making sure she had everything she wanted and encouraging her to talk—and talk. It wasn't difficult for her, she enjoyed conversation in any case, but by the time she was on her second glass of wine, all tension and inhibition had vanished. Jake asked her about her background, her family, her years at college and her subsequent employment as a designer for a big textile company in Yorkshire.

'It was a good job and I was quite well paid, but—oh, I don't know, it wasn't enough. Or perhaps it wasn't *right*. For me, I mean. It wasn't just that I wasn't doing what I really wanted to do, it was—well, my life didn't seem right somehow, there was something missing.'

'So you decided to change it. I admire that.'

'I'm not wholly certain I did the right thing,' she confessed. 'My family think I'm mad, but ... I wanted to do what I want to do, if you see what I mean. It isn't that I'm money-orientated.'

'That,' he said, with a shake of his head, 'I do know. And shortly I'm going to explain how to cost a job properly.' He took a notebook and pen from his pocket and placed them by his coffee-cup. The meal had been perfection itself, as she had already remarked to him. 'And,' he went on, 'I'll begin by pointing out that there's a difference between giving someone an estimate for a job and giving them a quote, a figure to which you are at least morally committed. But before we get down to business, tell me why you chose this part of the world. Why Salisbury?'

She didn't hesitate, she was so relaxed with him that she was able to tell him all there was to know about this, not that there was much. 'It's going to sound like a strange reason, but here goes. I'd only been to Salisbury once in the past, when I was eleven years old. It was during the summer holidays and I was on a coach tour with Mum and Dad and my three little brothers. That sort of holiday was all my parents could afford in those days, and it was hectic, now I think about it, dashing from one city to the next and sitting in a stuffy coach between times. Anyway, I simply fell in love with Salisbury on sight. We saw all the things tourists come to see, starting with the cathedral, and we weren't there long—but somehow it was familiar to me. I—it was strange, we'd be walking down a street and I would know what was around the corner.'

'And you were right?'

'Well, if that happened six times, say, I was right on four occasions.'

Jake leaned forward, interested, frowning, and without stopping to think she reached out her hand to put the tips of her fingers to his forehead.

'You're frowning again. Do you know how much time you spend doing that?'

'I do?'

'Mm. And it makes you look older.'

'Older than what?' he asked, trying not to smile.

Coralie laughed. 'Older than however old you are.'

'Thirty-five. Pretty old, eh, compared to you? How old are you, exactly? Twenty-one? Twenty-two?'

'Twenty-three.'

He shrugged. 'I suppose my twelve years' seniority makes me seem like a different generation.'

'Not in the least,' she said. He had caught hold of the hand she had put to his forehead, and the warmth of his fingers around hers was bothering her. Holding hands at a candlelit table in the corner of a restaurant seemed too...intimate. With him. Gently she pulled away and picked up her wineglass. She had declined his offer of brandy with her coffee, which was just as well. 'Where was I?'

'In Salisbury, experiencing *déjà vu*.'

'But that's the point, it seemed like more than that. It happened too often and went on for too long.' When Jake asked what else she would call it, if not *déjà vu*, she shook her head. 'I really don't know. Maybe I lived in Salisbury in a previous life.'

The smile that had been hovering on his lips broadened. 'I thought you were a dreamer, now I know it for certain.'

'You don't believe in that sort of thing?'

'I didn't say that. And take it easy,' he added, laughingly, laughingly but at the same time seriously. 'Do *not* climb on your high horse, I wasn't getting at you.'

'Then what do you mean when you say I'm a dreamer? What makes you think that, my negligent attitude to the price I ask for my work?'

'Among other things. The look you have in your eyes when you're painting, for one.'

She might have asked him his other reasons—and there again she might not—had he not gone on to talk business at that point.

When the bill arrived, discreetly enclosed in a little folder with the name of the restaurant on it, Coralie felt uneasy. When Jake did no more than glance at it, tucking a charge card inside the folder and handing it back to the waiter, she felt compelled to say something. 'It seems all wrong, Jake, your treating me to such a splendid dinner. I mean, it was all for my benefit. But if I were to insist that this is my treat, I would, frankly, find myself on the verge of bankruptcy.'

He couldn't suppress his laughter this time; she saw him trying—and failing. 'Ah, Coralie! You are as sweet as you are pretty, do you know that? Your lack of pretension is delightful. Even your cheeky wit is something I could get used to, at a pinch...'

'Cheeky wit?'

'I wanted to avoid the word sarcasm.'

In a poor attempt at an American accent she said, 'It's that bad, huh?'

'It's getting less frequent,' he told her, 'now that you've stopped being defensive with me. And by the way, this evening was not all for your benefit. I want you to know that it's been a very long time since I've enjoyed myself as much as I have tonight.'

It was her turn to be pleased, possibly inordinately pleased. She left the restaurant with her arm linked comfortably through his, feeling confident, and feminine, and respected.

She fell asleep on the way back to the bungalow.

It was the sound of the Jaguar's engine being cut that made her stir, vaguely wondering where she was, but not really caring. The last thing she remembered was the radio being turned on, the sound of soft music surrounding her.

'You may open your eyes,' an amused voice was saying, 'but there's no particular hurry. Any time within the next few hours will do—I'm quite happy looking at a lovely face with long, curling eyelashes.'

Coralie was smiling before her eyes came open. She was slumped down in the seat, her head resting against the soft leather upholstery, turned towards him. 'Now who's being cheekily witty? Or should I say wittily cheeky?' She peered at Jake with one eye, enjoying the sight of his darkly handsome face in the glow of the outside lights of his home. They were parked on the drive, next to her van, and it was with a feeling of dismay that she realised the evening was over and she had yet to drive home. She reached for the door-handle, but Jake put a restraining hand on her arm.

'Just a minute, Coralie. There's something——' He broke off, shaking his head, and the next thing she knew

she was being gathered into his arms. There had been
no warning; in her semi-stupor she had not expected this.
When his mouth closed over hers, she became fully,
startlingly, awake.

No one, but no one, had ever kissed her the way Jake
was kissing her. It began gently, slowly, his lips moving
against hers as if he were simply enjoying the taste of
them, the softness of them, and in spite of herself Coralie
responded with blatant encouragement. Her arms slid
around him and tightened, so she was closer to him, close
enough to feel the hard pressure of his chest against her
breasts. Jake's reaction was to kiss her more deeply,
parting her lips with the pressure of his own, sending a
signal of shock through her brain when he began to explore her mouth intimately, his tongue touching her
tongue erotically, then probing as if determined to know
all there was to know about this soft, moist part of her.

'Jake——' Coralie broke away perhaps too fiercely,
her heart hammering frantically, feeling as if all the
nerves in her body had been set on fire.

'Relax,' he said in tones of surprise. He was frowning
again. 'What is it? What's wrong?'

'I—it's time I made my way home.' She opened the
passenger door and got out, giving him no opportunity
to be the gentleman and open the door for her. She felt
gauche again, unsophisticated, but how could she tell
him his kiss had been shocking, affecting her more than
she would have dreamed possible?

'Coralie, wait a minute! What's the hurry? Come in
and have a cup of coffee with me.'

'No.' His hand was on her arm and she let it be, but
she did not want coffee, she wanted to go home. 'Thanks,
but it really has been a long day, Jake.'

'It has,' he conceded. 'So why not stay here with me
tonight?'

'What?' Shocked, appalled, she glared at him accusingly. 'What the hell do you take me for, Jake? If you think——'

'For God's sake!' He wasn't laughing, he seemed just as appalled as she. 'I might ask you the same question. I was only suggesting that we needn't drive back to Salisbury, that there are several beds here to which you are welcome.' When she looked at him blankly he added, 'Beds other than mine, dear child.'

'Oh.' She felt idiotic now. 'Well, that's...a kind thought, but no thank you. I'm going home and——'

'We,' he amended. 'I shall drive you home and I shall come for you tomorrow morning.'

'Oh, Jake, that's too silly for words. Why should——'

'Because I want to. Because that is how it's going to be. Because I suspect your ability to drive carefully, for one thing, not only because of the alcohol you've consumed but also because you're shattered.' With the quirk of an eyebrow he added deliberately, 'Much too tired to be made love to. Now, get back in my car at once.'

She did, knowing instinctively that argument would be pointless. And he didn't let matters drop as he drove her back to her flat, either.

'It might help to keep you awake if you consider one or two things,' he said drily. 'I want to put the record straight—again. Firstly, while this evening has been tremendously successful as far as I'm concerned, I did not have ulterior motives for asking you out.'

'Look, I'm sorry about the way I reacted. It's just—when you suggested—I thought——'

'I know what you thought. Which brings me to my next point. If I wanted to make love to you, Coralie, I would tell you so in as many words. I wouldn't make oblique suggestions about your staying the night in my home.'

She didn't answer that, she was blushing furiously, feeling grateful for the blackness of the country lanes down which they were driving.

'Furthermore, when I take a woman out, I do not expect her to drive herself home. Now, you might consider that old-fashioned or something, but that's the way it is. At worst, if I'd had a drink too many, I would put her into a taxi.'

'All right, Jake, all right. I shall consider that my legs have been very firmly smacked.' She shot a look at him and found he was silently laughing. Her attempt at lightness had succeeded and she was gratified; ending the evening on a sour note was the last thing she wanted.

Feeling more tired than she had in weeks, she thanked him for the lovely evening when he pulled to a halt outside her building.

His building.

'Since you're the man responsible for the design of this place,' she added, 'how come there are no security precautions at the doors?'

'They're flats for singles, in theory, built on the cheap. That was a question of the builder's budget. Come on, I'll see you inside. Have you been feeling spooked or something?'

'No,' she said honestly. 'I just wondered.'

He took her all the way to her front door, chatting as they walked up the stairs. He never bothered with the lift. 'Whether you stay in Salisbury or not, it was a good idea to buy rather than rent. The property market is quite healthy at the moment, and these flats will appreciate in value.'

'That's what I thought, that I couldn't lose.'

Jake took her key and opened up for her, handing it back with a smile. 'You thought of that all by yourself, did you?'

Coralie poked him playfully in the ribs—her fingers connecting with solid muscle. 'I might be a dreamer, but I'm not stupid. Well, not entirely!'

He laughed at her, with her, and said goodnight. 'See you in the morning. What time?'

'I don't know. Honestly I don't. Look, let me hop into a taxi—and charge it to your bill.'

'OK. Actually, I'll be working in the office in the morning, so that is a sensible idea. Goodnight, pretty one.' With that, and with the lightest of kisses on her nose, he was gone.

Coralie watched his retreating figure as he turned the corner to the stairs. He did not look back. She stepped into her hall and closed the door quietly, sighing deeply. Getting to know Jake Samuel was a very interesting exercise—she would never have believed how interesting it would be. She would never have believed things would go so far—all of it. Thinking back to that first telephone conversation with him, just a few days ago, was like thinking back over a matter of weeks. Such a short time and yet...what? She shook herself. Yet here she was standing motionless behind her front door, thinking about Jake instead of getting into her much yearned-for bed.

Unfortunately, sleep did not come as swiftly as it might have. While her body was tired, her mind seemed determined to go over the evening again, over conversations, shared laughter, over all the advice Jake had spelt out for her about her business, and, of course, over the way he had kissed her, the way he had held her, the way his body had felt, pressed against hers...

She had lost track of the time when she finally drifted off.

CHAPTER FOUR

THERE was a note on the kitchen table. Jake's hand-writing was bold, looped and easily legible. It read: 'Good morning, Coralie—assuming you get here before noon. I don't know when I'll get back from the office, but in case I miss seeing you, here's your cheque, taxis included. Thank you for everything, for last night and for all your hard work in getting finished in time for Stuart's homecoming. I'm sure he'll like what you've done, his father certainly does. I can see that you are as good as you think you are, and I can see also that you're capable of work far more demanding than rabbits and bears. (Not that there's anything wrong with rabbits and bears, I add hastily!) So I shall recommend you to any client, or anyone else, whose bill you might fit. Just be sure that the bill you give them fits accordingly. Jake.'

Coralie put the note and the cheque in her shoulder-bag, appalled at the feeling of dismay settling inside her. Quite what she had expected of today, her last day of work here, she did not know. She had expected to see Jake, not this morning but at least this afternoon... How long would he stay at the office, on a Saturday? And, yes, she had expected—well, she wasn't sure what.

But this was it, obviously, the end of a brief re-lationship, short and surprisingly sweet. Of course, it was for the best; she hadn't wanted to get involved with the man, not when his recommendation of her to others might depend on how well they got on at a personal level. It was better all round this way, that they had got to know one another enough to like one another, that he liked her work enough to pass on her name. Nevertheless, she felt flat.

She worked solidly through the morning and, to her own critical eye, quite satisfactorily. As usual she had no conception of the time, so it was with surprise that she looked at her watch to find it was almost five. At the precise moment of doing so, the bedroom door opened and in walked a plump, middle-aged woman.

'Oh! I'm sorry, lass, I—well, I saw this van outside and I couldn't think——' She broke off, staring at the wall on which Coralie was working. There was still a little way to go; the series of pictures she had done told a story without any words, and the woman was looking at it as if fascinated. 'Oh, but that's gorgeous! Stuart will love it!'

By this point Coralie had descended the ladder and was holding out her hand. 'I'm Coralie Dixon. Mr Samuel hired me to—are you Mrs Everly, his housekeeper?'

'Yes. I've just got back from my sister's and—oh, but this is so nice! Does Stuart know about it?'

'No, it's going to be a surprise.' Coralie couldn't help smiling, the woman was looking at her as if she had produced something magical.

'Whose idea was all this?' she demanded suddenly. 'It wasn't Mr Samuel's.' The smile had dropped from her face, leaving Coralie startled at the change in her attitude.

'Well, no. That is, yes and no. Painting the wall in the first place was his idea, but——' She broke off, gesturing and laughing. 'I suppose the outcome is down to Stuart himself, really. I just looked around and saw what he had in his room, you know, the books and toys and——'

'Thought so.' The housekeeper looked closely at her, nodded curtly and suggested she might like a cup of tea.

'I'd love one.' Coralie had no idea what to make of the woman; the expression on her face was a mixture of approval and disapproval, impossible though it seemed.

'Come to the kitchen, then. You're from Yorkshire, if I'm not mistaken.'

'And you're from Lancashire.'

'Yes, but I won't hold that against you.' Mrs Everly glanced over her shoulder, her eyes mischievous now. 'Maybe a sandwich wouldn't go amiss? How much longer before you're finished?'

'An hour or so. Two at the most.' Would Jake be back by then? 'Nothing to eat, though, thanks. I had a bit of lunch today, which I don't usually do, and I'm not hungry.'

They had reached the kitchen. The housekeeper turned to survey Coralie, and she concluded with a grunt, 'But you're just a scrap, there's nothing to you. What do you want to go skipping meals for? Who do you work for, anyway? I've never seen you before, have I? Do you live in Salisbury?'

They chatted for half an hour, which was more than Coralie had intended for her break. She told Mrs Everly who she was, what she was and where she lived—and Mrs Everly told her that she had been in Bournemouth with her retired sister, that it had been a smashing week in spite of mixed weather, and that she had not looked forward to coming back to work. 'Except for the little one, of course,' she added, her expression softening. 'Stuart's a lovely little boy. I didn't really want to take a holiday while he was in the hospital—but I suppose it was the obvious time to. I didn't want to leave Mr Samuel to fend for himself, either, not that he isn't capable. I left him plenty of stuff in the freezer. Shouldn't be surprised if most of it's still there, though.' She got up suddenly to fling the door of the freezer open. 'Thought so! He's been neglecting to feed himself.'

Coralie made no comment, feeling it would be out of order to respond to this lot. She asked only one question, tentatively at that. 'Have you—worked for him for long?'

'Since he got married. I started here when he and his wife got back from their honeymoon. That was ten years ago.'

Ten years. Why, then, did Coralie have the impression that Mrs Everly did not like her employer? How could that be? Why would a person work for, and live in such close proximity to, a person they did not like? 'I'd better press on,' she said. 'I must finish tonight, I believe Stuart is coming home in the morning.'

The housekeeper said nothing further. It was as if she had realised their exchange had been too revealing. She was worried about it, Coralie knew that for a fact when she was asked again where she lived. 'Did you say you live in town, Miss Dixon? You haven't been in these parts long, so I don't suppose you know many people yet?' Which really meant, Have I said too much? Will you gossip?

'Hardly anyone,' Coralie said deliberately, exaggerating somewhat. 'Just the people I've worked for.' She was smiling inwardly; while Mrs Everly might not be enamoured of her employer, she was a long way from wanting to lose her job.

So it *was* a strange household. Coralie had sensed it all along—she'd had so little to go on and yet she had known. The atmosphere in this house was wrong, all wrong.

She didn't see Jake. By seven thirty-five she had finished and was sitting on Stuart's bed, surveying her handiwork. She gave herself seven out of ten. Not too bad. She never gave herself ten out of ten. She glanced at her watch, admitting she had dawdled, that she had drawn out the last hour deliberately in the hope that Jake might come home. But he hadn't.

'Mrs Everly? I've finished. I'll be off now.' She held out her hand. 'It was nice to meet you. Maybe we'll bump into each other in town some time. Anyway, thank you for the tea.'

'Oh, but that's a shame! I mean, Mr Samuel not being here to see how it all ended up, not being here to thank you in person. Still, it's typical of him. He's a workaholic, let's face it.' She added the last remark as if she just couldn't help herself, though she tried quickly to cover for it. 'Of course, he is a very busy man. In demand, you know. He can't help it. He's kindness itself, really...' There it was again, that look of approval mixed with disapproval.

Coralie made the right noises and left.

It was almost noon when she woke up the following day. She leapt out of bed before remembering that it didn't matter, that it was Sunday and she had nothing to do. Maybe she would go in search of Sophie, perhaps they could go out and have lunch together?

She bathed and dressed, only to find that her neighbour was not in. She went back to her flat, her keys jangling on her fingers as she dashed inside to answer the phone before it was intercepted by her machine.

'Coralie? You weren't in bed, were you?' The voice was unmistakable, even though it sounded uptight.

'Is something wrong, Jake?'

'Not at all,' he said hurriedly, maybe too hurriedly. 'Stuart asked me to ring you.'

'Is he home? Is he all right?'

'Yes to both questions. He wants to meet you, he's over the moon with your mural, he tells me it's the nicest thing he's ever seen in the whole wide world.'

'The whole wide world, eh?'

There was no smile in Jake's voice. 'He's been pestering me to ring you all morning. I said it had to wait because you might be sleeping late after all your long hours.'

'I did. So what does he want of me?' she asked, wishing Jake had rung her simply because he had wanted to.

'That's just it,' he sighed. 'I don't know. He wants to say thank you in person, but there's also something he wants to ask you—and he flatly refuses to tell me what it is. It's top secret, apparently.'

Coralie didn't know what to make of this. 'And so?'

'So I'm ringing to ask if you could possibly drag yourself over here, only Stuart isn't fit to go out today.'

'Fully understood.' It was difficult to hide her pleasure, but she managed. 'You want—he wants me to come today?'

'If you can, if you don't mind. But if it's damned inconvenient, Coralie, just say so. You are not at the boy's beck and call.'

She glanced at the phone in her hand, frowning. Jake's tone was peculiar, as if he were cross with his child. 'It's no trouble at all, Jake. I have the afternoon free, so I'll come after lunch, if you like.'

'OK.' There was no enthusiasm. 'I'll give Stuart the news and perhaps that'll shut him up.'

Coralie said goodbye and put the phone down, thoughtful. Jake did not want her at his home, she was sure of it. But why? She thought back to Friday night and could make no sense in his change of attitude towards her. Friday had been so perfect . . . but yesterday there had been only that note from him, no sight of him, no telephone call. And now this.

She tried to shrug it off, but it wasn't an easy thing to do. Worse, she looked down at herself and made the decision to change from slacks to a skirt. Aware of the foolishness of it, aware of the hurt Jake's slight was causing her, she made herself a sandwich and changed nevertheless, opting for a white pleated skirt and an emerald green blouse. The green accentuated the green of her eyes, she knew, and the light make-up she applied did wonders for them. Satisfied with her appearance, if not her behaviour, she pulled on a jacket and headed for Grovely Wood, looking very incongruous in her old and battered van.

Stuart was in bed in one of the guest-rooms. 'I put him in there because I didn't fancy him sleeping in his own room until that paint smell's completely gone,' said Mrs Everly.

'Right.' Coralie nodded, beaming her friendliest smile at the housekeeper. There was no sign of Jake. 'Mr Samuel is working, I take it?'

The housekeeper seemed about to say something, changed her mind and looked away briefly. 'He's got a big project on at the moment, you know. He has no choice but to work today.'

When his son had just come out of hospital? Coralie looked keenly at the older woman, knowing she was thinking the same thought. She just didn't dare to say so, not after the remarks she had made the previous day. She had not expected to see Coralie again, certainly not in this house and so quickly at that.

'Are you Miss Dixon? Gosh, you're *pretty*! Daddy didn't say you were pretty.' This was Stuart's greeting. It sent Mrs Everly into gales of laughter—but Coralie only just managed to smile.

Something was tugging at her emotions and she didn't like it. Stuart Samuel was and was not like his father: his hair was sandy-coloured rather than black, but his eyes were Jake's in every way, as blue as blue could be and just as intense. And there was a wisdom in them that did not belong to a four-year-old. But the child looked tired, pale, and his throat was obviously still bothering him, she could hear it in his voice.

'So you're Stuart? Well, how do you do, young man?' To her surprise, Jake's son held out his hand formally, giving her a little nod as they shook hands.

'They won't let me sleep in my room till the paint's gone.'

'Till the smell has gone,' Mrs Everly amended. She had perched herself at the bottom of the boy's bed, indicating that Coralie should sit in an armchair.

'Well, that's only sensible,' Coralie put in. 'We want your throat to get better as quickly as possible, and paint smells can sometimes be irritating.'

'Daddy says I'm irritating sometimes. And I know what it means,' he added unhappily.

Coralie and the housekeeper exchanged glances, the latter looking embarrassed. She plunged in quickly. 'Oh, your father doesn't mean it, Stuart. He only says things like that when he's tired because he's been working hard.'

'But why is he always working?'

'We all have to work,' Coralie said smoothly, 'to earn money to pay for all the things we need.'

'But my Daddy's already got lots of money.'

This was not, absolutely not, what Coralie had expected. This...interview...was disturbing in the extreme. And where the hell was Jake? Why wasn't he in here, instead of leaving his housekeeper to it? His lack of consideration—for all three of them—angered her.

She plastered a smile on her face and rapidly changed the subject. 'I hear you like your new wall, Stuart.'

'It's the nicest murial in the world!'

'Mural,' the women chorused.

'Murial,' Stuart repeated innocently. He looked at Mrs Everly and said shyly, 'You have to go now. I want to talk to my new friend by myself.'

With admirable seriousness, Mrs Everly turned to Stuart's 'new friend'. 'I had been warned, Miss Dixon. Stuart made it quite clear he has something secret to talk about with you.'

Coralie nodded earnestly. No sooner had the bedroom door closed than she was relieved of her suspense. 'Miss—I want you to paint some clouds and birds for me—will you? Will you?'

'Clouds and birds? But there are clouds——'

'No. On the ceiling, I mean on the *ceiling*!'

'Oh!' Her mind was racing. What would Jake make of this? 'Well, Stuart, I don't really know.'

'Oh, *please*. My murial isn't finished, you see, not unless it goes on to the ceiling. Clouds are *always* over your head.'

'I—yes, I suppose they are.'

'And I know what kind of birds—seagulls! I mean, all those pictures, Paddington and the rabbits, they're all playing at the seaside, aren't they?'

They were if that was how he saw them. 'They certainly are.'

'Well, then!' In a gesture remarkably like one of his father's, the little boy held both hands open and shrugged. It was, it seemed, an end to the discussion. Like father, like son.

'Well,' she said brightly, but without letting the child think his wish was a *fait accompli*, 'I think the best thing to do now is to talk to your father.'

'You,' he said, his spirits dampening. 'You do it.'

'I intend to.' Coralie got up, smiling. 'I shall come back and let you know what's going to happen, Stuart. We'll just have to see, won't we? Now, you stay where you are, OK?'

'I will. Can I see your beads before you go?'

Coralie moved close to the bed and bent down. Her 'beads' were a single strand of cultured pearls, the best piece of jewellery she possessed.

Stuart took them gently into his fingers, rubbing his thumb along their smooth surface. 'They're nice.' He looked up at her, making her heart contract as he peered into her eyes with his intensely blue ones. 'You're nice, too.'

'And so are you.' She straightened, ruffling his hair, wishing she had thought to bring something for him. She would make up for that—if Daddy gave the go-ahead on the ceiling.

Mrs Everly was in the kitchen, unloading the dishwasher. 'I'm going to have a chat with Mr Samuel,' Coralie announced. 'I suppose he's in his study.'

'Yes, but—I'd better let him know.'

'He is expecting me, Mrs Everly.' Deliberately, she was deaf to the warning implicit in the housekeeper's hesitation. That Mr Samuel was not to be disturbed when in his study was too bad. 'I know my way, don't bother to show me, thank you.'

She knocked firmly but briefly on Jake's door and walked straight in. From the other side of the room a pair of angry eyes turned on her. Jake was sitting in the armchair by the window, smoking one of his very occasional cigarettes and doing nothing. Nothing!

'Forgive the disturbance, Jake, I can see how busy you are.'

'Coralie...' It was another warning, another one she was deaf to.

'Given that I came over here by special request,' she began, sticking her right hand on her hip and her left shoulder against his filing cabinet, 'I should have thought that the least you could do was say hello.'

'Hello.'

'In other words, I am offended.'

'Then listen——'

'Never mind,' she snapped. 'Jake, will you look at me, please?' He was, actually, but not at her eyes. He was giving her that familiar once-over, his gaze drifting from her legs to her hips to her breasts...and lingering there. 'Stuart wants me to paint clouds and birds on his ceiling.'

That brought his eyes to her face. 'Clouds and birds?'

'That's what I said to him—and with the same surprise. Yes, seagulls, to be precise.'

'Oh, by all means be precise.' There was a hint of a smile, but it did nothing to lessen Coralie's anger. Had Jake asked her to explain it, at this stage she would in fact have been hard pressed to. It was due to a series of impressions, not all of which were explicable. It was as if her heart knew something that her head could not yet make sense of. It was based on intuition, instinct, something like that.

'Your son has a lot of imagination, Jake. He informs me his "murial" is not complete, that since it's obvious that the bears and the rabbits are playing by the seaside, there should be seagulls. And another thing, it seems that clouds are *always* over one's head.'

'Well, I suppose there's no arguing with that!' He smiled fully then. 'You're looking particularly delicious today, Coralie. That skirt swings when you walk, it's very feminine.'

She ignored his compliments. 'So it's up to you, Big Daddy. Are you prepared to fork out more money?'

In one fluid movement Jake was on his feet, advancing on her. 'What? When I'll be——' He broke off, laughing at himself. 'I was going to say when I'll be hoist with my own petard. I'll have to pay through the eyes and nose, I expect.'

'Just a fair price, calculated according to the dictates of my business consultant.'

He smiled, looking directly into her eyes when he spoke, fazing her to the point where she couldn't hide her reaction. 'I didn't want to see you today, Coralie. I didn't want to see you yesterday, either.'

There was a momentary silence. She could feel a constriction in her breathing, more a sense of panic than anything else. 'Why?' she asked softly. 'Why not, Jake?'

'Because there's something about you, something that...changes my mood.'

'From what? To what?'

'Forget that.' He shook his head. 'Let me put it another way: you're altogether too distracting.'

'Distracting from what?' she asked, surprised by her own persistence.

It got her nowhere. Again Jake told her to forget it. 'Go ahead with the birds and the clouds,' he said, 'and send me your bill when you've finished. When can you start?' he added.

'I'm booked from Wednesday onwards, so any time the week after—or tomorrow and Tuesday if you'd prefer.'

'I'd prefer.' He took hold of her hand, the one that was perched on her hip. 'And so would Stuart; the sooner he can move back into his own bedroom the happier he'll be. And...Coralie, I apologise for my rudeness.'

She told him that it was forgotten, her attitude non-chalant. 'Let's go and tell your son the good news.'

Jake glanced towards his desk. 'You go ahead, I've got to get on with——'

Coralie wrenched her hand from his grasp, her eyes flashing. 'Jake, I insist you come with me!'

He blinked, clearly taken aback. 'OK, OK, it's not exactly a problem...'

They walked into Stuart's room together, and from that moment on Coralie watched the interplay between father and son with interest.

While she herself was not a parent, she had once been a child, and that was not so long ago that she had forgotten what it was like. Stuart was both in awe of his father—and also afraid of him. His seeking of permission, his seeking for *approval*, was such that he could not relax and be himself. At least, the Stuart she observed in Jake's presence was not the same little boy she had chatted with.

The child's glee at his father's go-ahead for the ceiling was muted; only his eyes showed real enthusiasm. 'Thank you, Daddy. Miss Dixon wanted to do it for me, but she thought she better talk to you first. Isn't that right, miss?' He turned to her for support.

'My name is Coralie,' she told him. 'But if that's too difficult, you can call me Corrie.'

'No, I can say it. Coralie, Coralie! It's a pretty name.' He turned to his father, a touch of accusation in his voice. 'You never told me she was pretty.'

'Didn't I?' Jake said, as if surprised at himself. 'Then it's clever of you to reach the same conclusion.'

Stuart wanted to know what 'conclusion' meant, but Jake seemed to have lost patience. 'I'll explain later,' he said, getting up. 'I have to talk to Coralie now, so say goodbye.'

Quite why she leaned over to kiss the child, she wasn't sure, she knew only that she wanted to see Jake's reaction as well as Stuart's. The boy flung his arms around her neck and hugged her... while Jake looked on with a frown.

The frown was gone by the time they were at the front door. 'There's just one proviso, Coralie...'

'Proviso?' She had no idea what he was talking about.

'To this latest commission. The artist must have dinner with me tomorrow.'

'I'm sorry, the artist has a date tomorrow evening.'

'A date? You—never mentioned there was a man in your life.'

'You never asked,' she countered. 'But my date isn't with a man, it's with my neighbour, Sophie. A girls' night out.'

'I see. Tuesday, then?'

'I don't know.' She said it because she really didn't know. Whether she wanted to have more time alone with Jake was something she would have to think about now. 'Ask me on Tuesday.'

She drove home in a state of confusion, half wishing that today, the phone call from Jake, had never happened. Stuart did have a lot of imagination, bless him, but if he'd had a little less Coralie would not have heard directly from Jake again, she felt certain of that. He had admitted wanting to avoid her, today and yesterday, and the only reason he had given was that she changed his mood, was too much of a distraction. From his work, presumably. Yes, that was it. When his housekeeper had referred to him as a workaholic it had been no surprise to Coralie; she had gleaned that much long since, since the time he had first phoned her and had assumed she worked on Saturdays, as if everybody worked on the weekend.

Sophie was home when Coralie got back. She'd been out for lunch with a man, a new acquaintance who had told her in so many words that if she were not prepared to go back to his place and make love, there was no point in their seeing one another again.

'Bloody nerve!' Tall and attractive, if a little too thin for Coralie's taste, Sophie moved around the flat like a tigress. She had come in search of Coralie several times during the past couple of hours—had almost pounced on her when she'd got back from Jake's. 'I had less than two hours in his company and that was that. I mean, really!'

Coralie looked sympathetic. 'He certainly put his cards on the table——'

'You can say that again. Honestly, I have the most rotten luck with men. I'm twenty-seven and I just don't seem to grow any wiser where they're concerned. I don't know what's the matter with me.'

There was nothing the matter with her. Sophie was divorced, but not from the want of trying to hold her marriage together; her husband had been persistently unfaithful to her, till it had reached the point where she could stand it no more.

'I mean, you can't just go jumping into bed with people these days,' she went on, still prowling around. 'It's far too risky. In any case, what sort of girl did he take me for? This was our first date—and I'd thought him such a gentleman! You can never tell, you know. They're all the same basically, sex is always the first consideration with men.'

Coralie glanced down at her hands, thinking about Jake, about the exchange they'd had when they got back to his bungalow last Friday. What if she had reacted differently, if she had said yes when he'd suggested staying the night? Would he have refused, if he had realised that she thought she was accepting an invitation into *his* bed?

Given Sophie's mood, Coralie shouldn't have talked to her about Jake, but she did. She told her everything there was to tell because she felt the need to. She regretted it later.

'Would he have refused?' Sophie said scornfully. 'My God, you're even more innocent than I thought! I mean, look at you, what man would refuse to go to bed with you? I don't think you misunderstood Jake at all, I think he was trying it on. He sounds just like the rest of them to me—a bit more subtle, perhaps.'

'Sophie, you *are* biased, face it.'

'If you didn't want my opinion, you shouldn't have asked for it.'

Which was true. 'Well, I'm not at all sure you're right.' Coralie got up to make more coffee, feeling depressed. 'He did say that if he wanted to make love to me, he would say so in as many words.'

'And you believed him? It doesn't work like that. Unless you get an ultimatum of the type I've just had, the process is an insidious one. Wait and see what happens on Tuesday—if you do decide to go out with him again.'

Coralie had already decided she would go out with Jake, because it was more than she could do to refuse. Why should she, anyway? After all, he was just as free as she was. She wondered again about his wife, about the sort of marriage he'd had. Stuart was only four; Jake's wife might have died quite recently and—and maybe he wasn't over it yet. Was that why he had wanted to avoid her, because he didn't really wish to get involved with another woman?

He was at home the following day, Easter Monday, and for most of the time he was working in his study.

Coralie was subjected to a dozen interruptions while she worked during the morning—by the boy whose ceiling she was painting. Both she and the housekeeper kept shooing him out of the room, explaining that he shouldn't be in an atmosphere of wet paint, but it was pointless. Stuart kept popping in and out just the same, excited and eager to see how his clouds and birds were coming along.

It was around lunch time when Jake caught him chatting to Coralie and hovering in the doorway. She heard the stern tones of Jake's voice coming down the corridor.

'Stuart? What are you doing in there? Back to the other room at once!'

'I'm not in here,' the boy protested. 'I'm only standing in the doorway!'

'Don't answer me back, Stuart. Scoot.'

He scooted. Jake came into the bedroom and looked up, apologising for his son's interruption. 'I'll bet he's been pestering the daylights out of you.'

'Not at all.' Coralie was perched on the top of a high step-ladder, craning at the ceiling. 'I can talk and work at the same time.'

'Then talk to me.' Jake stretched out on Stuart's bed, looking up at her, his hands behind his head. 'How's your neck holding up to all that?'

'Well, ceilings aren't my favourites, I will admit.'

'Then it's just as well you'll be stopping for lunch shortly. I've just had the five-minute warning from Mrs E.'

'Lunch? But I don't——'

'Try telling my housekeeper that. She's one of the older generation, doesn't understand people wanting to skip meals, especially young things who are still growing.'

Askance, Coralie turned to stare down at him. He started laughing uproariously. 'Not my words, pretty one, I was quoting.'

'Good grief! How old does Mrs Everly think I am?'

'Sixteen, probably. Can't say I blame her—with that ponytail and your tomboy clothes, you don't look any more than that.'

She shot him a dark look. 'Don't just lie there watching me work. Get hold of this, will you? If I *have* to eat lunch, I must clean up a bit.' She handed Jake the tin of paint she'd been using. 'Just dump it on the floor, I'll put the lid on it.'

He did as she asked, turning to catch hold of her around the waist as she came down the ladder. They wobbled precariously when he lifted her off and swung her down to the floor. 'Jake, you idiot! Be careful!'

Jake ignored her protest, she was locked in the circle of his arms and he pulled her close, hard up against the length of his body. 'I've been seeing your face on my drawing-board all morning,' he told her softly, 'haunting me, taunting me. It does nothing for my concentration. I think there's only one way of exorcising it.'

That was her warning of what was to come, but she didn't try to escape him. Her mouth met his willingly, opening under the warm pressure of his lips. He kissed her with no gentleness this time, it was as though he had meant what he'd just said, that he wanted merely to get this out of his system, rid himself of the distraction she represented.

Maybe he would have if the kiss hadn't lasted as long as it did, but once he was started Jake seemed determined not to let go of her. When she made a move to free herself, his arms tightened, a small groan escaping him. 'No, you don't!' He spoke against her mouth, his lips moving to her cheeks, her temples, her closed eyes.

The feel of his body told her what he must surely be thinking, that this had not been a good idea, after all. His arousal was shockingly fast, making Coralie's heart beat wildly with a mixture of excitement and fear. It gave her an unprecedented feeling of power, knowing she could have such an effect on Jake. She was also afraid that Stuart or Mrs Everly might walk in.

'Jake, let me go.'

He didn't, he raised his head and looked into her very green, very bright eyes. 'Why? You want this as much as I do.'

'No.' She glanced towards the door. She didn't want this, not here, not now, and not like this—not when there was an element of punishment in his kiss. It had felt as though he had been kissing her almost against his will.

'Yes, Coralie.' He caught hold of her chin, bringing her eyes back to his. 'This has been there all along, from the instant we first set eyes on each other. Despite the way we clashed, beyond anything that was said, you were attracted to me. As I was to you.' He gave her no chance to deny it, he proved his point by kissing her again, gently now, his mouth moving against hers with tantalising lightness. A second later he was kissing her neck, his mouth working downwards until his lips were pressed against the hollow of her throat.

Coralie murmured his name involuntarily, feeling sure her bones were melting. In the firm security of his embrace it would have been so easy to give in, to relax her body against the solidity of his and just enjoy what was happening, what he was doing to her. Never before had she felt such desire for a man, such a need to kiss and be kissed, to touch and be touched . . . but when Jake's hand moved to her breast it served only to alarm her further.

'Jake, please! Someone might walk in——'

'So what?' His hand slid to her breast regardless, his mouth claiming hers once again, hungrily now, exploring as deeply as he had last Friday. When at length he raised his head, they were both breathless, hearts pounding, looking at one another with a kind of shocked understanding.

It was Jake who spoke first—when Coralie averted her eyes. 'You're blushing again. Why? And what if we were seen? Is kissing you a crime, Coralie?'

'No, I just—I was considering your four-year-old son.'

'Let me worry about Stuart. Come on, let's go and eat.'

Coralie escaped into a bathroom, needing time to compose herself. What was happening to her? Her hands were shaking, the reflection in the mirror didn't look like her, her eyes were too bright, almost wildly so, the pink fullness of her lips telling of the way she had been so thoroughly kissed. Nor did it end there. Her feelings for Jake held more than physical attraction, she had to admit it, but she was damned if she could say how much more...

'I'll be going to the big school soon,' Stuart informed her at lunch. The three of them were in the dining-room, not at the kitchen table, and Mrs Everly was popping in and out, seeing to their needs.

'The big school?'

'In September,' Jake explained. 'He'll be five by then.'

'Ah, I see!' Coralie gave the boy a broad wink. 'Bet you'll love it at the big school, mm?'

'Bet I will. Daddy, when is my birthday? I've forgotten.'

Jake's eyes were on his food, he did not look up. In a voice that was not his own, he said, 'It's the fourteenth of May, Stuart. You ought to remember your birthday by now.'

Coralie flashed a look at him, resentful of his tone. How many children of such tender years could rattle off their birth date? Stuart was a bright boy but he didn't know when May was—his next question told her that much.

'Is it long to my birthday?' As if determined not to annoy his father again, he had asked Coralie.

'Now, let me see, where are we? It's April the——'

'It's next month,' Jake put in.

'Which probably doesn't mean a thing to him,' she pointed out, looking at Jake defiantly. 'Time is an unknown quantity when you're Stuart's age—or have you forgotten?'

He stared at her. 'Oh, excuse me. Pardon me for breathing. Yes, actually, I have forgotten. I'm very old, remember.'

'Yes, you are,' Stuart agreed happily, oblivious to the undercurrent. 'But Mrs Everly is even older, she said so. She's going to be sixty soon.'

'Who's going to be sixty soon?' The housekeeper was just in time to catch this, her eyes twinkling. She was clearly crazy about the boy, Coralie noted with satisfaction, which was just as well because the same could not be said for his father. Jake seemed to have a low threshold of tolerance as far as his son was concerned. Or maybe she was reading too much into things? A moment's thought reminded her that he wasn't the most tolerant of men in any case. Even with her he had hardly been the epitome of patience. Or there again, maybe especially with her...

'I go to school now,' Stuart was saying, 'but it's only playschool and I think it's pretend, really. I'll learn more at the big school. You did say so, didn't you, Daddy?'

'I did.'

'And it's a very, very good school,' Coralie was informed. 'Daddy has to pay to let me go to it.'

Her reaction to this was mixed. So Jake was at least determined to give his son a fine education, but did this mean he would end up at a boarding-school? 'What sort of education did you have?' she asked, turning to Jake.

'The usual sort. Prep school, boarding-school, university. I did four years at Oxford.'

Coralie bit back a smile. All that privilege! Was that what Jake considered 'the usual sort' of education?

Stuart put his knife and fork down. 'Can we be excused now, Daddy?'

'May,' he corrected, 'You mean, *may I be excused*.'

'No, I mean me and Coralie. Can we be excused?'

Distracted from matters of grammar, Jake looked at his son with interest. 'You and Coralie? You have plans or something?'

'She said she'd have a game of snap with me today.'

'When I've finished my work,' Coralie put in hastily, glancing at Jake.

Behind him, just reaching to take his empty plate, was Mrs Everly. She caught Coralie's eye and glanced heavenward when Jake said, 'Right now, I'm going to have words with Coralie myself.'

The child looked uncertain. 'But—you will play cards with me, Coralie? You promised!'

And a promise to a child was never to be broken if it were humanly possible not to do so. She had always been of that opinion, having experienced many broken promises herself as a youngster. 'I did and I will, Stuart, just as soon as I've finished my work for the day.'

Delighted, he scurried off—only to be called back by his father. *'Stuart!'*

'Yes, Daddy?'

Jake made his point firmly. 'You were not excused from the table. Now, however, you are. You may go.'

Coralie glanced again at the housekeeper, feeling as uneasy as the older woman looked. 'You wanted to talk to me, Jake?'

'In the drawing-room.' He turned to Mrs Everly. 'We'll have coffee in there as soon as you can manage it.'

'It's ready now, Mr Samuel.' She retreated. Jake got to his feet.

Coralie went with him to the big living-room, vaguely amused because she was about to be put on the carpet for some reason. 'Words?' she said, the instant he closed the door behind them. 'You wanted to have *words* with me, Jake? What have I done now?'

He gave her a half-shrug, motioning for her to sit. 'It's something and nothing. I'm wondering——' He broke off because Mrs Everly came in with the coffee-tray. She set it on the table in front of Coralie. 'Will you pour, Miss Dixon?'

'Thank you, yes. And please call me Coralie.' She didn't hold with such formality herself. It was different for Jake, he was the woman's employer and, after ten years of living in such close proximity, it probably suited them both to maintain a little distance. Alone again, she glanced at Jake and asked him to go on.

He seemed to have changed his mind. 'It doesn't matter.'

Coralie took his coffee over to him. 'It does matter. Say it, please.'

'All right, I didn't care for the angry glares you were giving me at lunch. Over Stuart.'

'The business about his birthday? But you were so snappy with him! I mean, he's only four. I couldn't under-stand——'

'Then don't try,' he said, in tones far snappier than he had used with his son. 'Don't try, Coralie, because my relationship with my son is none of your business.'

She was staggered, so much so that tears sprang to her eyes. Rapidly she turned away, reaching for her coffee-cup. 'I'll have this in Stuart's bedroom, if it's all the same to you.'

'It isn't. Stay here. I want——' When she kept right on walking, he growled after her, *'Coralie, come back here!'*

She didn't dare turn around, the tears in her eyes would be visible. 'Get lost,' she flung over her shoulder. 'I'm not four years old, I don't have to wait to be excused!'

Convinced he would pursue her or at least growl again, she was both surprised and relieved when there was no explosion. He was angry, she knew that much, but he was seemingly content to let matters rest.

It was not until six o'clock that she saw him again. At four, Mrs Everly popped her head round the door, announcing that tea was up. 'And some freshly baked scones. I'm sure you'll be able to manage a couple of those?'

Coralie trailed into the kitchen after her, laughing. 'Mrs Everly, if I spend much more time around here, I'll be as big as a house.'

'Never! You don't mind if I sit with you, do you?'

'Of course not. What about Mr Samuel's tea?'

'He's got it. He's having it in the study.'

'And Stuart?'

'Watching one of his videos in the living-room. His father bought several to keep him entertained till he goes back to playschool. Next week, thank goodness.' She shook her head wearily. 'Much as I love the mite, he is a handful. I'll be sixty in June, and if truth were told

I'd like to retire and go and live in Bournemouth with my sister.'

'Oh! I hadn't realised your sister lived there. I thought you'd both gone there for a holiday.'

'No, no, Elizabeth retired there several years ago. She's older than I am, also a spinster, and she'd worked hard all her life. Mind you, she has a good pension. Not that I'll be short when I retire,' she added, pushing scones, butter and jam in Coralie's direction. 'Mr Samuel's taking very good care of me. He's a generous man but— oh, I don't know.'

'What? What do you mean?'

There was a hesitation, just a slight pause during which Mrs Everly looked carefully at the younger woman, wondering whether she could be trusted. She lowered her voice, glancing in the direction of the door. 'I shouldn't be saying this to you, but what Stuart needs is a mother, not a sixty-year-old housekeeper.'

Coralie smiled. 'It's funny, I had the impression you wouldn't want to leave your job here.'

'I do and I don't. For myself I do, very much so. I've had enough, I've got arthritis and it doesn't get any better as time goes on. But I worry about Mr Samuel, which I know is silly. It's just that he changed so much, he's not at all the man who employed me ten years ago. He used to be—well, people do change, don't they?'

It was difficult not to fire a dozen questions at her. Coralie kept an impassive face and waited, hoping answers would be volunteered anyway. Some were— some, but not all. Mrs Everly said that Stuart was her main reason for staying, that Mr Samuel was more than capable of looking after himself, even if he would ne-glect to eat at times. 'But he'd be no good with Stuart,' she added. 'Not if he were alone with him.' She lowered her voice further, shaking her head. 'And I wouldn't

like to leave the two of them alone. You've noticed how
Mr Samuel is far too strict with the boy. He's a stickler
for discipline.'

That wasn't the trouble. Coralie's upbringing had been
strict, in her case it had been her mother who had laid
down the law. There was nothing wrong with discipline
in a child's life. 'Does Mr Samuel know you want to
retire?'

'No!' There was alarm in her voice. 'Oh, dear me,
please don't——'

'Not a word.' Coralie held up a hand. 'Of course I
shan't say anything, to him or to anyone else. Please
trust me, Mrs Everly. And tell me, please, what happened to Stuart's mother?'

The housekeeper looked surprised. 'She died. Did you
think Mr Samuel was divorced or something?'

'No, he told me he's a widower. But how did she die?
When?'

'In childbirth. She died shortly after Stuart was born,
on the fourteenth of May five years ago.'

In childbirth! Coralie might have known, she should
have guessed. 'That's—I'm very sorry to hear that.'

'That's when Mr Samuel changed. Overnight, in fact.
Of course it was an awful shock to the poor man, to
everyone, but he's never been the same since. He never
used to be impatient, surly, like he is now. He's never
been involved with another woman since, either. He's
never even looked at one. Not to my knowledge,
anyhow.'

Mrs Everly was a terrible gossip. Coralie thought with
a shudder what Jake's reaction would be if he knew the
half of what his housekeeper was saying. And to a
stranger, because the older woman had no idea of
Coralie's relationship with Jake, if it could be called a
relationship. Maybe that was why she was talking so

freely, because of that ignorance. She was also frustrated, torn between wanting to retire and having to stay for love of Stuart, her sense of duty towards Jake. 'So I can take it that his relationship with his wife was a good one?'

'A *good* one?' The housekeeper threw up her hands. 'Oh, heavens above, yes! They were so much in love, every bit as much as they had been when I first started with them, the day they got back from their honeymoon.'

CHAPTER FIVE

'YOU'RE not letting him cheat, are you?'

Startled, Coralie looked up to find Jake standing in the doorway. She was sitting cross-legged on the floor of the guest-room with Stuart, giggling like a schoolgirl. 'Certainly not! We're neck and neck.' She glanced at the sets of cards they both had. 'When he beats me, he beats me fair and square.'

'Coralie drew some cartoons for me.' Stuart leapt to his feet, eager to show his father the sheaf of papers on which she had been drawing. 'Look at them, Daddy, look!'

Jake obliged, sifting through the various Disney characters. 'They're very good.'

'They're wonderful! And they all have their own stories. Coralie told me the stories while she was drawing them for me.'

'I'll bet she did.' Jake looked down at her sprawling figure, she was lying on the floor now, with her head on her hands. 'Just like I told you, Coralie, you're a dreamer.'

It wasn't criticism, the smile tugging at the corners of his mouth told her that. He was amused, his attention once more on the drawings. 'You were right, Stuart, they're more than good.'

'Wonderful,' the child insisted. 'I told you. And so is Coralie!' As if to prove it, he dashed over to her and promptly sat on her.

She squealed in protest, turning over to catch hold of him. She started tickling him until he was helpless. 'Is that any way to treat someone wonderful? Mmm? Come on, speak to me, speak to me!'

He couldn't, he was in stitches. Jake hadn't moved, the drawings were still in his hands, but he was watching the goings-on with an expression bordering on disbelief.

'Did you want something, Jake?'

'I—it's time for Stuart to eat. It's six o'clock, and Mrs Everly is waiting to feed him.'

'And then I play for half an hour and then I have my bath and then Daddy tells me a story in bed—but you can tell me a story tonight, Coralie.' He turned to Jake. 'Coralie doesn't need to read stories out of books like you do; she can make them up.'

'I can't say I'm surprised,' Jake said drily. 'Off you go to the kitchen, Stuart.'

'Wait a minute.' Coralie didn't want the child to think she was staying. 'Stuart, I have to leave in a few minutes. I can't tell you a story tonight.'

'Oh. Do you *have* to go?' At her nod, he looked crest-fallen. 'Well, what about tomorrow? When you've finished my ceiling, can you stay longer and tell me a story?'

Coralie looked helplessly at Jake. She had expected him to intervene, but on this occasion he hadn't. He was grinning, looking at her as expectantly as his son was. In the face of her prolonged silence, he said quietly, 'Well, what about tomorrow?' Which meant what about our dinner date?

She nodded, glancing at Stuart's eager face. 'I'll bring a change of clothes with me.'

'You don't have to do that,' the child assured her. 'I like your old clothes.'

When Jake finished laughing at the remark, he sent his son to the kitchen and turned to Coralie, his expression sobering. 'You've really made a hit with Stuart.'

Did he mind? She couldn't be sure. 'He's made a hit with me.'

Jake hesitated. 'I take it your date with Sophie is still on for tonight?'

'It is, and I really must go.'

'A pity.' At her questioning look he added, 'I mean, you would have been welcome to eat here tonight.'

Mrs Everly said the same thing when Coralie went through to say goodnight. 'You're going? What a shame! Mr Samuel thought you might like to eat with him.'

So it had been Jake's idea, not his housekeeper's. 'Some other time, perhaps, thanks all the same.'

'Like tomorrow,' Jake said pointedly, addressing the older woman. 'It isn't one of your whist nights, is it? I'll need you to babysit, if you don't mind. I've asked Coralie out to dinner tomorrow.'

Mrs Everly was clearly taken aback, though not at all displeased. 'Oh!' Her eyes went straight to Coralie's, questioning and worrying. 'Of course I'll babysit.'

Wishing she could put her at her ease, Coralie smiled reassuringly. 'See you tomorrow morning.'

Jake walked to her van with her, she got in and wound the window down. ''Bye, Jake.'

'Hang on. I—listen, I'll be in the office all day tomorrow, I have a series of meetings, so if Stuart's a nuisance tell Mrs Everly firmly to keep him out of your hair. I don't want——'

'He won't be a nuisance! Good heavens, haven't you noticed? I find it very easy to relate to children.'

'Yes,' he smiled, 'yes, I have noticed. I'd have to be blind not to.'

When Coralie went through the grand finale of her story to Stuart the following evening, someone tapped quietly at the door. A second later Jake was in the room.

'I missed the ending,' he said, his face wreathed in smiles.

'What?'

'The ending. I missed it. I've been listening outside the door for the past fifteen minutes, but every time you lowered your voice, I missed a bit.' He glanced away from her to his son, laughing at the look of horror on her face.

'I don't believe you!' she squeaked. 'Jake Samuel, you were *not* listening!'

'Was, too.' He was grinning like a Cheshire cat. 'So what happened to the wicked witch?'

'She vanished!' Stuart filled in the end of the story for him, repeating almost word for word what Coralie had said—but far more loudly. 'But she didn't die, she just went back to the place where she really lived, on another planet.'

'Ah! A happy ending all around, then. So settle down, Stuart, and be very good. Coralie and I are going out now and I don't want you giving Mrs Everly any trouble at all, do you understand?'

'No,' came the guileless reply. 'I don't understand, Daddy. If you and Coralie are going out, does it mean you've got a date?' He glanced at the story-teller, wanting to make sure he understood this new addition to his vocabulary. 'A date, like the princess had with the soldier, when the king didn't know about it?'

'That's right. It's very much like having an appointment, and you know what that word means, don't you?'

'It's what Daddy does when he goes to his office—he has appointments and meetings.'

Jake smiled at that. 'I do other things at the office, too, but yes.'

'Well, the soldier and the princess had dates because they loved each other. Do you and Coralie love each other?' Stuart added hopefully.

Neither of them knew where to look; Coralie studied the carpet and Jake cleared his throat. 'I think that's more than enough questions for tonight, Stuart. Settle down now, off to sleep.'

'Daddy!' When Jake made a move to leave, the boy reacted with something close to panic. It brought Coralie's head up with a snap. 'You didn't kiss me good-night! You forgot to kiss me!'

Her heart sank at the desperate importance Stuart attached to this—not that it was surprising. She had seen how undemonstrative Jake was with his son, and she did not doubt that kissing the boy goodnight was the most he ever did to show his affection.

When Stuart had kissed Coralie as well as his father, giving her a very prolonged hug, she and Jake left the room. He slid an arm around her waist the instant the door was closed, and she stiffened, feeling resentful towards him.

He sensed it at once, he also misunderstood it. 'What's up?' he laughed. 'Are you cross with me for eaves-dropping? I didn't want to come in and inhibit you, which I might have.'

'You would have.' She meant it, she was feeling idiotic about that business, but the real reason for her resentment was something she couldn't talk to him about. At least, not yet.

Jake smacked her lightly on the rump. 'Go and say goodnight to Mrs E, little dreamer. I'll be with you in a few minutes.'

The housekeeper was watching television in the living-room, a glass of sherry in her hand. She had made her curiosity known to Coralie earlier in the day, having been both perplexed and pleased when she had referred to her date with Jake.

'You're still worrying,' Coralie said now. 'Please don't. Everything you've said to me was strictly between you and me.'

'So you've said, lass, but I didn't know it was like...like that...with you and Mr Samuel. And this isn't your first date with him, he mentioned——'

'It isn't "like" anything,' Coralie cut in. 'I'm sure his taking me out is just a reward for my hard work here.'

'Are you?' Mrs Everly managed a smile both cynical and pleasant at the same time. 'Oh, I do hope that isn't the case! Look, love, I'm not saying this for my benefit but for yours: if I were you, I wouldn't mention his wife's death unless he does.'

Coralie almost laughed. 'I wouldn't dream of it, believe me.'

An hour later she was asking Jake where he was taking her. They had driven to Fordingbridge so he could drop off a parcel at his sister's house. Coralie had no idea what it contained, nor had she set eyes on Jake's sister, she had waited in the car on the road at the bottom of the drive. Jake had left the engine running and had been gone for precisely three minutes.

He glanced at her quickly, shifting the gears to second to take a tight bend. 'Are you starving? Sorry about that diversion to Jean's, it took us a bit out of our way.'

'That's OK, I'm just curious as to our destination.'

'We're eating at the Amberley Inn, where the food is excellent. It's pretty basic, but very good indeed. It has a relaxing atmosphere and I'm sure you'll like it. It's much less formal than that place we went to last week.'

Coralie did like it; it was a country pub and restaurant, and their speciality was steaks. She had in fact been there before, on one of two dates she'd had with

a man who had turned out to be married. The memory
of him didn't sour her enjoyment in any way, it merely
amused her because the man had lived to the north of
Salisbury and the Amberley Inn was about fifteen miles
to the south—far enough, he had no doubt thought, for
him not to be spotted by anyone who knew him.

'Coralie? I said what would you like to drink?'

'Sorry, I was miles away.' She and Jake had settled
by a fireplace in which logs were burning, throwing a
warm and cosy glow into the bar. She told him what she
was thinking about, and what had happened. 'I've been
here before, Jake, and you're right about the food and
the atmosphere. I wasn't going to mention it because . . .'
She paused deliberately, amusing herself. 'I was here with
a married man.'

'Were you, indeed? I wouldn't have thought that was
your style.'

'It isn't, I didn't know or even suspect he was married.
Furthermore, he was happily married.' She burst out
laughing. It was a full minute before she could say anything else. 'It was really very funny. We were in the bar,
just over there, and we'd just given our order to the
waitress. My date was busily chatting, flattering me,
when—would you believe it?—his *wife* walked in!' She
was off again, laughing and shaking her head at the
memory. 'With another man!'

Jake covered his face with his hands, joining in with
her laughter and muttering about embarrassment.

'But he wasn't embarrassed, that's the point—he was
furious because he'd caught his wife out with someone
else!'

'So what happened?'

'I was forgotten, abandoned. He and his wife left at
once, arguing madly. I couldn't hear what was being said
because I stayed where I was, out of it.'

'And the other man?'

'He stood by the bar, gaping at them. Then he came over to me and asked if he could buy me a drink. I said no, but if he could possibly drive me to Salisbury, I'd be grateful.'

'And he did?'

'Of course. He didn't have anything else to do, did he?'

'And did he know? I mean that he was out with a married woman? Did you ask him?'

'Certainly, that was too much to resist. He knew all right—and he was married, too.'

Jake sobered, shaking his head. 'Then none of them were happily married. Not him and not your chap, either. You were wrong about that.'

'No. The other man told me that the wife had told him very firmly that she and her husband were happily married.'

Jake wouldn't wear it. 'Ask yourself a question, Coralie. How could she be, if she was seeing someone else? All right, maybe she was *reasonably* happy, but not totally. There was something missing, something she had to find elsewhere.'

'Well, I suppose you're right,' she conceded. 'But it's a very common ailment, and it seems to me that totally happy marriages are very, very few and far between.'

'They're not all that scarce.'

She looked directly at him, making up her mind to act on this perfect cue. 'Was your marriage a good one? Fulfilling, I mean?' She held her breath, half sorry she had asked the question, wishing she could name the emotion that flashed in his eyes. There wasn't time— Jake glanced down at the table, and when he looked at her again he was smiling.

'Very much so. It was one of those few and far between, as you put it. Now then, you never told me what
you'd like to drink.'

The subject of marriage, his or anyone else's, was at
an end. Jake went to the bar, and when he came back
he mentioned that she would be getting a telephone call
from a man named Southworth, a photographer friend
who had been looking for someone like Coralie, someone
who could do some painting with a difference in his
home.

'His wife is delightful—very outspoken, like you.
You'll get on well with her.' His blue eyes were twinkling, looking devastatingly attractive as they teased her.
'And Tom Southworth says she knows exactly what she
wants doing.'

'Namely?'

'I didn't ask, I just said you were the person for the
job.'

Coralie was laughing again. 'I see! Well, thanks for
the show of confidence. And, Jake, thank you for
helping me. I mean it.'

'My pleasure,' he smiled. 'My confidence in you is
enormous, you see.'

She was about to speak, but someone beat her to it.
From behind, a beautifully spoken female voice said, 'I
can't say the same for my confidence in you, Jake
Samuel. You *idiot*!'

Jake turned round so fast, the drinks on the table
almost got knocked over. 'Jean! What the devil—why
didn't you say you were coming here?'

'Why didn't you?' his sister countered.

It had not been difficult to guess who this was. Jean
and Jake were very much alike physically; she had the
same mop of jet-black curly hair—albeit much longer—
and very similar eyes. Coralie was introduced to her

without further ado, and to her husband, Greg Adamson. A minute later all four of them were seated by the fire and Jean was admonishing her brother.

'You never mentioned you were on your way out. And what were you thinking about, anyway, leaving Coralie out there in the car?'

Jake held up a hand in defence. 'My darling Jean, *you* said you were going out, so naturally I had no wish to detain you.'

'Don't give me that. It wasn't till you dropped in that you knew I was going out.' Realising at once what she had said, she turned to look carefully at Coralie. 'Which tells its own story, doesn't it? He simply didn't want to introduce you to me. Now, why is that, Coralie? I'll tell you why. It's because you are *not* a business acquaintance of my brother's.'

Coralie looked swiftly at the man by her side, but it was Greg who spoke up, not Jake. 'Jean! Will you please behave yourself? You're not content to put this lovely young lady on the spot, you won't even give her a chance to answer your potentially embarrassing question!'

'Sorry.' Jean was appropriately subdued. 'Curiosity got the better of me.'

'So we observe.' There was irony in Jake's voice. He gave Coralie a sympathetic smile before turning back to his sister. 'For one thing, jumping to the conclusion that I didn't want you to meet Coralie is a nonsense. For another, she *is* a business acquaintance.'

Dismayed at what she saw as renunciation, Coralie watched Jake watching his sister. He gave her a few seconds in which to digest what he'd said before adding, 'However, she does happen to be rather more than that, and maybe, just maybe, I wanted to keep her all to myself for a while. Consider that. Also, for the record, both of you, I met Coralie exactly one week ago, almost to the

hour, come to think of it, and I've brought her out tonight to celebrate that happy occasion—so if you have
any ideas about joining us when we eat, forget them.'

'*Well!*' said Jean, while Greg, utterly delighted by this
speech, threw back his head and roared with laughter.
Jean joined in almost immediately, so did Coralie. This
was no renunciation, this was a very positive acknowledgement as far as she was concerned. How Jake might
define their relationship privately she had no idea, but
he had made it clear to his relatives that she was special.
He was looking at her now as if to confirm it, for all to
see.

'Good for you, Jake!' Greg was saying. 'But don't be
mean, share Coralie with us tonight.'

'No chance. Some other time.' As if on cue, the
waitress came with the menus, taking in the situation.

She addressed Greg, asking if it should be a table for
four. A swift glance at Jake told the older man he had
meant what he'd said. 'No. Two tables for two, thank
you.'

Coralie heard and saw all of this, managing at the
same time to answer the questions Jean fired at her. 'No,
I'm from Yorkshire. I'm a decorator.'

Jake took over; he seemed determined to protect
Coralie and it amused her no end. She let him explain
what she did, and she laughed aloud when Jean went
into raptures. They all chatted for about twenty minutes
before they split up.

Fortunately their respective tables were at opposite
ends of the restaurant. 'Thank goodness they're way over
there,' she said to Jake. 'It would have been too silly if
they'd been put next to us.'

Jake smiled. 'I saw to it that they weren't.'

Coralie cast a glance in the direction of the waitress. 'You devious man. But I wouldn't have minded, you know. Greg and your sister are lovely people.'

'They are, very much so, but if you knew how often it has been hinted to me that I should remarry, you would understand why I don't want them to jump to any false conclusions.'

It was surprisingly difficult for Coralie to react to that, difficult for her to keep her voice casual. 'Meaning you'll never remarry?'

He shrugged, busying himself by rearranging his cutlery more neatly. 'Never is a very long time, Coralie. I didn't say never. But if I ever do decide to marry again, it will be entirely my own idea, not someone else's.'

It was time for a change of subject. 'Have Jean and Greg got any children? I never asked——'

'Three. Boys of nine and seven, a girl who is precisely Stuart's age. Jean and my wife got pregnant at——' Abruptly he stopped, leaving Coralie to finish the sentence for him, which she did.

'Jean and your wife got pregnant at the same time.'

'Yes. But my wife died as a result of her pregnancy, very shortly after giving birth to Stuart.'

There was a silence. Coralie sought frantically for something to say quickly. 'I'm very sorry to hear that, Jake. And you—I have the feeling you've never got over it.'

'Alison's death? Yes, I have. It took a long time but—well, it's been almost five years now.' He looked into her eyes, smiling. 'It's all right, I really don't mind talking about it, so don't worry. Alison's death was one of those things that are never supposed to happen. She was young and fit and strong...but she died.'

Another silence. Tentatively, she thanked him for telling her and added, 'I had wondered, Jake. There are no photographs of Alison in your house, and I thought that very strange.'

'Strange? Not at all. That's for Stuart's benefit. I put every photograph away after she died.'

Coralie was aghast. She had to wait while the waitress set soup dishes before them and went away. 'Stuart's *benefit*? Jake, how can you say that? How can it be to his benefit?'

'For heaven's sake!' he snapped, as if she weren't using her brains. 'The boy knows he had a mother, a mother who's no longer with us. What would be the point in reminding him of that, of having her photographs on view?'

'It might be a comfort to him.' She kept her voice low but steady, her eyes directly on his. She could see anger in their blue depths, but she couldn't, wouldn't, keep quiet. 'You amaze me. Can't you see that the absence of any pictures is like—well, it's as if you've forgotten Alison and you would choose for Stuart to forget her too.'

'Stuart never knew her,' he said tightly. 'Your soup's getting cold.'

'That's all the more reason,' she persisted, 'to have Alison's face on view, so he can know what she looked like. He's bound to be curious. Has he never asked to see a picture of his mother?'

Jake was no longer looking at her, his eyes were elsewhere when he spoke, his voice barely audible. 'Dammit, *no*. He has *not*.'

Coralie had to let the subject drop, she was only too aware of his seething anger, and knew that she was in danger of ruining the evening. But she had to have the last word, she just had to. 'Then it's only a matter of time,' she said firmly. 'One day, he will.'

They ate in silence for a while. Coralie's food was no doubt excellent but her exchange with Jake had robbed it of any flavour, it tasted extraordinarily bland. From time to time she looked up at him, and whenever she did so he was watching her, his expression gauging, weighing, as if he were doing an entire re-think about who and what she was.

At length she smiled, determined to break the atmosphere. 'I'm beginning to feel like a worm under a microscope. But I'm not squirming, Jake. I'm entitled to my opinions, and if you don't like them it's tough luck.'

It seemed that a full minute passed before he answered, before he co-operated in easing the tension. When at last he spoke, he was smiling that full and devilishly attractive smile which made Coralie's heart skip a beat. 'So it seems. My tough luck, as you say. It seems to me also that the only way to stop you voicing your opinions is to gag you.'

What came over her then, she did not know—she simply found herself flirting outrageously. 'Oh, come on, Jake!' Her eyes were wicked, challenging, looking more beautiful than she could know, reflecting the light of the candles on the table. 'I happen to know you've got more imagination than that.' She let her eyes drop to his mouth, feeling gratified when she saw a wry twist to it.

'My God,' he muttered softly, 'what a thorn in my side you are, Miss Dixon. What a provocative and deliciously tempting distraction!'

The evening was salvaged; for several minutes the two of them were aware only of one another, there were no other diners in the restaurant and the atmosphere had become one of mutual appreciation.

'I'm sorry to interrupt.' Greg appeared, touching his tie self-consciously and looking vaguely embarrassed.

'But Jean wants to know if we can at least have coffee together later.'

Coralie bit her cheeks, seeing that Jake was having difficulty in not laughing, too. When her eyes told him that this was fine by her, he relented. 'We'd be delighted, Greg. I suppose I can share Coralie for the last half-hour or so.'

'So your parents live in Bermuda?' On the way home Coralie remembered something Jean had said about her having had a letter from her parents. She had referred to them as lucky dogs, sunning themselves daily in Bermuda.

'My father worked there for several years, with a bank. When he retired he decided to stay. He and Mother love the place, the life there, they have dozens of friends and, of course, decent weather. Can't say I blame them.'

'Nor I! Do you miss them?'

'Yes and no. They've been away for so long, I just accept it. But they miss me and Jean, and most especially their grandchildren. I take Stuart out there every year so they can see how he's doing.'

She smiled at the warmth in his voice. It was quite obvious that Jake's relationship with his parents was a loving one; she only wished she could say the same thing about his relationship with his son. 'I miss my mother,' she volunteered, 'even though it was only Christmas when I left home. She's a good friend, so is Dad in a different sort of way.'

'And your brothers?'

'Monsters, all of them! Noisy teenagers whom I do *not* miss. Well, not much....'

Jake drew the Jaguar on to the forecourt, laughing softly at her. 'I don't believe that, of course you miss them.' He walked around the car to open the door for her, his eyes sliding along the length of her legs as she swung them out and stood.

She was doing it again, looking up at him with mischief in her eyes. 'Why, of course you believe me, Jake! Have I ever lied to you?'

'Minx!' He caught hold of her chin, his other arm closing tightly around her waist, urging her closer. 'I doubt you would spare anyone, even yourself, with lies.'

'You give me too much credit. I have been known to withhold the truth, which is akin to, if not quite the same as, lying.'

'It's the same.' His eyes were twinkling in the lamplight, roaming over her face admiringly. 'So you must have suffered a temporary aberration.'

'Aha! More sarcasm, Mr Samuel. Your voice just lowered an octave.'

It amused him no end. 'There could be another reason for that,' he pointed out, inching her body closer to his. 'Come on, let's go inside, I'm gasping for a decent cup of coffee—for one thing.'

The coffee in the restaurant had not been good. Jake had sent it back with polite but firm complaint. The second cup had been just as bad, though.

Coralie needed time to think about the wisdom of being alone in her flat with him . . . in the circumstances. She was far from unaffected by his nearness, she was yearning to be kissed, but she was grateful also that he hadn't kissed her in view of anyone who happened to be watching from the building. She eased her way out of his arms, chattering as they started to walk, knowing he would insist on seeing her to her door in any case.

'I've wondered whether it really is a virtue,' she said, 'telling the truth. I mean, it's got me into trouble plenty of times and—it can hurt, too, even though they say the truth never hurt anyone.' When they reached her front door she dug out her key and handed it to him; he opened up and gestured for her to precede him, flicking on lights in the hall.

'And there's something else, too,' she said over her shoulder. 'It's often a question of——'

That was as far as she got. Jake's hand closed on her arm, he spun her round and gathered her impossibly close. 'What's the matter, Coralie? Why are you so nervous?'

'Nervous?' she said nervously, 'I'm not——'

'Now you are lying.' Jake wasn't amused, he was frowning, at a loss to understand her. 'Surely you're not afraid of me?'

'Of course not!'

'Then what is it?' A light dawned in his eyes, a slow smile started there and spread to his mouth. 'Is it this?' His kiss was devastating, different again, lasting so long that she thought, and hoped, it would never end.

When he lifted his head to challenge her, he made no pretence of being unaffected himself. His deep voice was gentler than she had ever heard it, his eyes closing briefly as he told her precisely how things were. 'God, you're exciting! I want you, Coralie, and you want me. Don't tell me you're afraid of this when it's so *right*!'

'Jake, I . . . please let go of me. I can't think when I'm so close to you.'

'Don't think,' he urged, 'just *be*.' Then his lips were moving against hers again, shocking her into further arousal. One hand had slid to her breast, his thumb brushing over the tell-tale stiffness there.

'Please, Jake!' She wrenched away with a mixture of guilt and the nervousness she had no intention of denying any longer. Again his need of her had made itself known, and she couldn't handle it, couldn't handle him. Jake was an intensely passionate man, and it had been a mistake to flirt with him the way she had. He hadn't needed that sort of encouragement, he wanted her and he was now telling her so in plain and simple English.

'Coralie, I want you, right here and now. I want to make love to you for the next several——'

'Don't! Please, Jake, I—can't cope with this. You move too quickly, far too quickly.'

There was a low rumble of laughter. 'Too quickly? Too quickly for what? What do you mean?'

When he took a step towards her, Coralie took a step back, shaking her head. '*Don't!* You don't understand that it isn't so straightforward, not for me. I won't deny I'm attracted to you, strongly attracted, but unlike you, I don't feel that this is right.'

For seconds he merely looked at her, his narrowed eyes intent on hers before, seemingly satisfied with this further information about her, he shook his head slowly. 'All right. I can accept that. You want me and yet you don't want me. I'm not unfamiliar with that feeling myself.' He gave her a wry smile, his hands coming up in a gesture of defeat. 'I fought my attraction to you at first—but yesterday lunch time I gave up on that. So, go and make us some coffee, little dreamer, but remember this: it isn't going to go away. I want you whether you're in my presence or not, and if it isn't the same with you, it soon will be. Believe me.'

She believed him. She went into the kitchen feeling disorientated to the point where she couldn't remember which cupboard the coffee was in. A part of her seemed to be standing outside herself, looking on and smiling wisely. It was an odd sensation, knowing with her heart that what Jake said was true...and knowing with her brain that all he really wanted was her body.

CHAPTER SIX

DURING the weeks that followed, Jake disproved what Coralie's brain had told her. At first it was always at his instigation that they met; not once did he part from her without fixing another date, whether it was one day or several days ahead. As her confidence in their relationship grew, she invited him and Stuart to lunch at her place on Sundays, which was Mrs Everly's day off, and they always stayed till around five in the afternoon.

She and Jake fell into a pattern of seeing one another four or five evenings a week, and on days when Coralie wasn't working Jake would ring her from his office to ask her to join him for lunch, which was usually at the Red Lion. It had been at the Red Lion, over afternoon tea, that Coralie had met Mrs Garner, the then stranger who had recommended her to Jake. They confessed to having a soft spot for the charming, centuries-old coaching inn because of that.

Coralie's confidence continued to grow when Jake put no pressure on her. When she was in his arms and she called a halt, he neither argued nor pressed the advantage they both knew he had: she wanted him and it was only a matter of time before he would have her. They both knew that, too.

'I hardly see anything of you these days,' Sophie complained one morning when she and Coralie happened to be leaving their flats at the same time. 'I'm lucky to get a cup of coffee with you at the weekend. You're always tied up with tall, dark and handsome.' She had met Jake and Stuart one Sunday when she had called to borrow some sugar, and she was now asking what it was with Coralie and Jake. 'I mean, where is this affair heading, exactly?'

It was a good question. 'I don't know,' Coralie confessed. 'And it isn't even an affair, as such.'

'You're joking! Come on, Coralie.' Sophie shook her head in amazement. 'No, you're *not* joking. Then for goodness' sake . . . you couldn't give me a lift to the town centre, could you?'

'As it happens, I can. Come on. You'd better let me back my van out of the garage first. It's getting very cramped in there.' The single garage was stuffed full of planks and trestles, paintpots and brushes; it was getting to the stage where she would have to rent something, another garage at least. 'Thanks to Jake, I've got as much work as I can handle these days. And the grapevine is working wonders.'

'But you still have days off.' Sophie climbed into the van, shoving a stack of sketchpads along the bench-seat to make room. 'Quite apart from weekends.'

'Too right I do.' Coralie smiled. She was in the fortunate position of being able to choose which jobs she took on; if someone asked for something that didn't appeal to her, she simply said she was booked for weeks ahead. It usually made them look elsewhere. She hadn't done a plain painting job in all the time she had known Jake. 'I don't intend to work myself into the ground, that was never the idea. I have more than enough for my needs and I like my free time. I'm very lucky.'

Sophie slid a sideways look at her. 'How about answering my question? The one about you and Jake.'

The younger girl sighed. 'I did. I don't know the answer, Sophie. I don't know where this relationship is heading. She narrowed her eyes against the glare of the sun when she turned a corner, thinking aloud. 'I like him far more than is good for me, probably, and the more I get to know him, the more I like him. He's a very positive person with positive ideas——' She broke off, keeping to herself that which she did not like about Jake. It was a drawback, a shortcoming in his character of which he was not himself aware, and it was not to be talked about with Sophie.

'You were saying? A very positive person—and?'

'And I adore his sense of humour, too. It's strange really, because when I first met him I thought he didn't have one—but he can be so witty, very dry at times, almost silly at other times. We often giggle over things like a pair of kids.' She shook her head, still marvelling at the discoveries she had made about Jake. 'But when he's serious, he's serious, intense even. Yes, very intense. We can talk about anything and everything, although he loses me when it comes to politics. Needless to say, he's got very firm views on——'

'Needless to say,' Sophie cut in, laughing, 'you're in love with the man.'

Coralie looked at her quickly. 'Yes, I—oh, Sophie, I think I am.'

'Well, don't say it as though it's the end of the world!'

'But . . .'

'But what? Oh, I see. He doesn't feel the same way, right?'

'I don't know.' She had no idea how Jake felt. That he liked her and was both happy and content in her company was obvious, but never had he mentioned the word love. 'He's never said anything remotely pertaining to . . . to love.'

'And have you?'

'No. No, I haven't.'

Sophie advised her very strongly not to. 'For heaven's sake, don't frighten him off, then. It might be enough to make him freak out.'

The dramatic expression brought a smile to Coralie's lips, but her friend was right, of course. If she were to tell Jake how she really felt about him, it would probably be the end of what was, so far at least, a beautiful friendship. Despite what he'd said, Jake was not entirely free of the effect his wife's death had had on him. In one way he was over it, in another he was not. 'I'm sorry, Sophie, what did you just say?'

There was a grunt. 'You have got it bad! I was asking if you'd come shopping with me on Saturday, I have to find an outfit for that wedding I'm going to, and I've left it long enough as it is. It's only two weeks away.'

'Oh, I'm sorry, really I am, but I'm committed. Stuart's having his fifth birthday party on Saturday and I've promised Jake's housekeeper I'd get there early to help her.'

'Oh. Well, that's that, then. Just assure me you'll give me your opinion on what I end up with. I haven't got your good taste when it comes to clothes. If you hate what I buy, promise you'll tell me so I can take it back.'

'I'll tell you, that's a promise. And stop doing yourself down, will you? I've yet to see you wearing something that really doesn't suit you.'

Coralie dropped her friend off and drove on rather slowly, her thoughts very firmly on Jake, as they so often were. It was different now, though; actually saying that she thought herself in love with him had made her focus on her situation. No, there wasn't any doubt, she was in love with him all right, and it frightened her.

'So, who's the man in your life?' Coralie's mother wanted to know. She woke her daughter by ringing at six-thirty on the Friday morning, apologising and insisting she had been left with no choice. 'I've phoned you and phoned you, left messages you're obviously deaf to on that machine of yours.'

'But I only spoke to you five days ago, Mum!' Coralie yawned loudly. 'Anyway, it's OK, my alarm's set to ring in fifteen minutes.'

'That's not relevant,' Anne Dixon insisted. 'That we spoke five days ago, I mean. You fobbed me off then when I asked who was taking all your spare time—are you going to fob me off now as well? I hope not, because instinct tells me that something's wrong. Is he married, is that it?'

Coralie sank into an armchair, smiling. This was typical of her mother; she knew her only daughter better than anyone else in the world did, including Jake, and it was amazing that this conversation hadn't happened before now. 'Not married, no. You know me better than that, Mum. He's a widower with a son, Stuart, who's just five.' Her eyes went to the small dining-table in the corner of the room; on it was the mobile she had been making for Stuart's birthday. It was a series of seagulls in flight; she couldn't think of anything that would please him more, he had toys galore, he went short of nothing—materially.

'Jake's a bit older than me,' she went on. 'Thirty-five. He's an architect, he's very successful and extremely intelligent. He's also——' She broke off, she had to take care not to enthuse too much, the way she had to Sophie. 'Well, let's just say I like him a lot.' In the face of her mother's silence she asked jokingly, in broadest Yorkshire, 'Now what are you whittling about?'

'I'm wondering if I'll get to meet him, Coralie?'

It was Coralie's turn to be silent. That was a loaded question if ever there was one. 'Oh, I don't think so, Mum. No, I don't think so.'

'But you've made noises about coming home for a weekend soon. Why not bring him with you? And the boy, of course. What are their names again?'

'Jake Samuel, and his son is Stuart. He's a precious little boy, and I know you and Dad would love him but—his father's so busy with his work, you see. In fact, he was a workaholic before——'

'Before what? Go on. Before he met you? Is that what you were going to say?'

It was what she had been about to say. Things had changed, though. Jake found time, made time these days, for her, at least. Mrs Everly had remarked on the change in him, so had his sister, Jean. Coralie had done some work for Jean the previous week, in her children's rooms, and she too had mentioned the change in Jake. A change for the better, she had said. It had been almost embarrassing at one point, the way Jean had gone on so, because with it there had been open curiosity in her eyes. It seemed that everyone wanted to know what was going to happen with Jake Samuel and Coralie Dixon.

'Well,' she said laughingly to her mother, 'let's just say that I manage to lure him away from his desk now and then.'

There was another silence. 'Coralie, you haven't been doing anything...too risky, have you?'

'Risky?'

'You know very well what I'm talking about, our Coralie. Like risking an unwanted pregnancy, for starters.'

'No, Mother.'

Anne's voice softened. 'Don't use that tone, love, it's a natural question for a mother to ask. I'm sure your Jake is a nice, respectable man but—well, you might be twenty-three, but I still worry about you.'

'I know, Mum. Sorry if I sounded snappy. Oops! There goes my alarm clock. Do you want to hold on while I switch it off?'

'No. I can hear your father moving around upstairs, I'd better start breakfast. Ring me soon, though, won't you? Shall I give Dad your love?'

'Of course. I love you both. I love the monsters, too. I'll even give you permission to tell them so. 'Bye!'

At her end of the line, Anne Dixon replaced the receiver gently into its cradle. The girl had changed; in five short months she had changed a great deal. Anne didn't need to see her daughter to know that. So, there was a man in her life and it was serious. Well, there was nothing for it but to rely on the girl's intelligence, considerable intelligence, and hope and pray she would not end up being hurt in any way.

'Mrs Everly? Hi! What a rotten day for a party. I'd hoped it would be sunny so we could shoo all the children into the garden after the first hour or so. Where's Mr Samuel? I thought he'd be in here helping you.'

'You must be joking! He'll probably hide in his study for the entire afternoon. He's already remarked that children's parties are not his scene, not that I needed telling.'

Coralie grinned and set to work.

At three-thirty the children started arriving in droves. Jean and her brood of three had got there a little earlier, thank goodness; that meant there would be four adults supervising—when Jake emerged. Jean was staying to help out, while all the other mothers handed their children over with happy smiles and quips about having freedom for two or three hours.

By four o'clock there was still no sign of Jake. Coralie went to root him out of his study. 'Jake?' He was surrounded by papers, a pencil was tucked behind his ears and a frown of concentration was tucked between his brows.

'Just coming, sweetheart.'

'You'd better, we *need* you!'

He turned to look at her, taking her seriously. 'Is it that bad?'

'No! The worst comes later—when they've finished eating and the games begin.'

It was when the games began that the trouble set in. Stuart was over-excited, loving being the centre of attention. He was rowdier than Coralie had ever seen him, to the point where she had to go over and whisper to him, telling him to settle down.

She spoke for his ears only, giving him a quick cuddle. 'Darling, you're showing off. Now, calm down and let the others have their turn. Go on, pass the parcel quickly, you can't win every time just because it's your birthday!'

She moved away, keeping a close eye on him. A squabble had broken out only minutes before—and Jake was clearly simmering, not at all thrilled with his son's performance.

Coralie went over to him and slid her arms around his waist. 'Take it easy, Big Daddy, they're *all* over-excited.'

He did not hug her in return, he stated that he was not interested in what they *all* were, he was interested in what his son was doing. 'I haven't brought him up to show off like that. I can't think what's got into him.'

'Nothing's got into him, only the party atmosphere.' From across the room her eyes met with those of Jake's sister. Jean was in charge of the music, but she was looking worriedly at Coralie.

That was how Coralie missed seeing the accident, the glass of milk which went flying off a table to splatter all over the carpet. All she heard was Stuart's, 'That's not *fair*, Peter rotten Johnson! You snatched the parcel out of my hands—and look what you made me do!'

Since Mrs Everly was busy wiping jam from someone's face and Jean was determinedly keeping the game going, it was Coralie who dashed into the laundry room where the cleaning cloths were kept. When she emerged, neither Jake nor Stuart were around.

'Give that to me, lass.' Mrs Everly held out her hand for the cloth, jerking her head in the direction of the living-room. 'You'd better go to the rescue before he wallops the lad.'

Coralie didn't think, she just acted, cutting swiftly through the dining-room to the living-room. At least Jake had taken Stuart out of earshot of his friends.

The boy's lower lip was trembling, he was making a determined effort not to cry as his father lectured him in no uncertain terms.

'I know it's your party,' Jake was saying, 'but that does not give you the right to cheat! What the devil's got into you? You're five years old and you know better than that. I shall have no more of it, Stuart. You will play fairly or not at all.'

'But I *was*...' The reply was uncertain, guilty, and Stuart's eyes went straight to Coralie for support.

She smiled. 'Were you?' she asked softly. 'Really, Stuart?'

λ

'Well...I just kept thinking the music was going to stop.'

Jake shook him. 'Stuart! You will either——'

'I think he's got the message, Jake.'

He ignored her. He was still shaking the child, not hard, but unnecessarily. Definitely unnecessarily. There were tears threatening in Stuart's eyes, and Coralie feared an outburst. It was all she could do to hold her tongue as his father went on lecturing.

Throwing a tantrum was the worst thing Stuart could have done, which was precisely what he did. His tears didn't materialise, his temper did. 'Leave me alone!' he yelled in his father's face. 'You're always picking on me, just because you don't like me to have fun!'

Jake spoke the boy's name, just once, and the warning in it made Coralie flinch. She jumped in with both feet.

'Jake, he has got the message. You're making matters worse, winding him up. Can't you see that? Let him go back to the party now, please. Jake——'

He was glaring at her icily, struggling to control a temper that was now aimed at her. He turned to Stuart and nodded, keeping his voice low. 'Off you go.'

'It's no *good*!' the child shouted. 'They'll all know you've been telling me off and they'll laugh at me. They'll think I'm a baby!'

That, at least, Jake handled well. 'No, they won't,' he said in the same quiet tones. 'I very carefully brought you in here so you would not be shown up in front of your friends. Now, go back to them and play properly.'

Coralie stepped aside to let the boy pass. She was about to follow him, but Jake stopped her. '*Hold it!* I want words with you and I want them *now*!'

She exploded. 'Words, Jake? I've told you be- fore——'

'And I've told you before, what goes on between me and my son is nothing to do with you! Remember that from now on. Things are bad enough with you as they are.'

'Bad enough? What the hell is that supposed to mean?'

Jake's eyes were like flint, his voice an angry, low-pitched roar. 'It means that Stuart is so crazy about you, he's turning to you more and more for support.'

'So what's wrong with that? God knows, he needs some!'

He took two threatening paces towards her, wagging a finger at her. 'Discipline, Coralie, discipline! You don't seem to know the meaning of the word. A child needs it, even wants it.'

She stood perfectly still, watching him carefully as she spoke. Her words took the wind out of his sails, but she felt no satisfaction, no triumph. 'I agree with you, I agree with you wholeheartedly. But a child needs love, too, and as far as Stuart is concerned, you don't know the meaning of that word.'

He stared at her. 'You'd better explain yourself.'

'Damn right I will! You resent that child. Don't look at me like that, Jake, I happen to be telling you the truth.'

'You happen to be talking a lot of——' The word he chose was a measure of his fury; she had never heard him swear like that before. 'Why the hell should I resent my own son?'

'Think about it,' she came back rapidly. She was shaking with anger at his blindness. 'Not once, not *once* have I ever seen you pick him up and cuddle him. And it can't be any different when I'm not here, I know it isn't. The only show of affection that child ever gets from you is a perfunctory goodnight kiss. That's all. There are no hugs and cuddles, and if you think for one moment that he doesn't notice that, think again. He's always——'

'Oh, you haven't finished yet?' Jake cut in, his voice dripping sarcasm.

'I haven't even started! You haven't got the first clue about balancing discipline with love, Jake. Stuart is forever telling me how Daddy never plays with him, how he and Daddy don't go out and do things together—as his friends do with their fathers. And what do *I* say to this sort of thing, what do *I* do? I make excuses for you, that's what I have to do! I make excuses which must sound pathetic even to the ears of a child! You're not the only busy man in town, you know. You can find time for me, so why not for Stuart?'

'Supposing you tell me,' he said acidly, 'since you obviously know it all.'

Coralie did just that. 'All right. You resent Stuart because he killed Alison.'

Jake froze. For long, endless seconds he was immobile. Suddenly he turned his back on her, his voice no more than a stunned whisper. 'God in heaven! What a terrible thing to say!'

Her eyes closed briefly. Anger had given way to fear—but she wouldn't stop now. 'Yes, it is. And the sad thing is, it's true. In your eyes, Jake, in your eyes. And that is why you resent your son.'

When he said, very, very quietly, 'But I do love him, Coralie,' she thought her heart would break. The need to go over and hold him close was awful, awful because she did not dare. She was afraid he might turn on her again...and she still had a few more things to say. She looked at the rigid line of his back, loving him and hoping desperately she would be able to get through to him. 'Darling Jake, I'm sorry, but it is true. You told me you were over Alison's death and I believed you. I still believe it. But that's strictly as far as you yourself are concerned. It's high time you forgave Stuart now, for what you see as his responsibility. I know you love him, of course you love him—one would have to be inhuman not to. But it's your very humanness that's created this gulf between you. Certainly there should be discipline in his life, the authority of a father who won't be manipulated, I agree. Of itself that's a source of security for the child, but it's not enough, it's not *enough*, it has to be tempered with love. Stuart needs to know without a shadow of a doubt that you love him regardless, that your love is unconditional. As things are, there's no balance, there's no—— '

'Christ! Lay off, will you?' It came out more wearily than angrily, but he still would not turn to look at her. 'I suppose you'll tell me next that Stuart needs a mother?'

'No. Not necessarily. Not if he can have you, *all* of you. You can provide for all his needs, Jake, not just material, not just disciplinary, but everything.'

The silence that followed stretched on interminably. Coralie stood with her heart in her throat, convinced he would tell her to get out of his house. He didn't, he simply asked her, finally, to leave the room. 'Would you mind leaving me alone? I need to think.'

She got out of there at once.

She was shaking when she rejoined the party, oblivious to the fact that everything was running smoothly. Jean was at her side in a flash, and, without thinking how she was talking out of context, Coralie told her that she had just given Jake a piece of her mind. 'I mean . . . I mean about his relationship with Stuart.'

Jake's sister was impressed, her eyes widened and she nodded slowly, looking at Coralie as if she were proud of her. 'Then good for you. I've tried to do that and

I've had my head bitten off, severely bitten off. Thank God someone has been able to get through to him.'

Coralie was by no means sure she had. She looked at Jean with frightened eyes.

The older woman smiled. 'But you're not just anyone, are you? Listen, I want to tell you something. As far as I'm aware, Jake has had two affairs since Alison's death, both during the past eighteen months. They were never made public, they were very short-lived and they wrought no change in him. But you have. I only hope—well, I think you can guess what I hope for, Coralie. I hope my brother has the sense to recognise what he has in you.'

Coralie looked away. 'Jean, I want to go home now. I can't stay here any longer, not just now. I feel——'

'That's OK.' Jean's hand reached for hers, squeezing it reassuringly. 'I understand. Slip away before the lord and master comes back. I'll explain about your rotten headache.'

By the time Coralie got home her headache was not a matter of fiction; her temples were pounding and her heart felt like lead. How was Jake going to react to all she'd said—if he reacted at all? If she ever saw him again . . .

She lay down on her bed, too weary to take off her clothes. She felt drained, not even hoping to sleep, just to rest. But sleep came, surprisingly, and when next she opened her eyes it was dark outside.

Shaking herself awake, she looked at the clock. It was only just past eight; ahead of her was a long and unpleasant evening during which she would, inevitably, worry herself sick. She was already worrying, convinced she would never see Jake again. She had gone too far and he would not tolerate that kind of interference.

She slipped out of her clothes and ran a hot bath before making a mug of coffee. Her movements were desultory, like those of one who was decades older, and it was with an acute sense of depression that she carried her coffee into the bathroom. Tomorrow was Sunday, and she dreaded it. There would be no Jake, no Stuart here for lunch and an afternoon of fun. Jake wouldn't even ring her to cancel, he wouldn't want to talk to her at all. She had walked away this afternoon, away from the party and away from him, and he was not going to ring her.

Nor did he. He turned up on her doorstep instead. By then it was getting on for midnight, but Coralie was still up, huddled in her dressing-gown and staring unseeingly at the room in general.

Her reaction on seeing him was peculiar: she was swamped with relief, certain that her heart would burst from sheer love of the man, and yet she could not greet him enthusiastically. Her greeting told only of all the uncertainty, all the fear she had been feeling. 'Jake, I . . . didn't expect to see you again.'

He smiled at that, an odd mixture of pleasure and sadness. Gently, he put a hand under her chin, lifting it so she had no choice but to look at him. 'I'm here to ask you to marry me,' he said.

CHAPTER SEVEN

'YES, I am serious,' Jake said softly, before she had a chance to accuse him of not being. 'I've never been more serious in my life.' He smiled into her eyes, his hand was still under her chin and neither of them had moved at all. 'I've done a lot of thinking this past few hours, not only about my relationship with Stuart but also about my relationship with you. *Our* relationship, Coralie.'

'And what...oh, let's go inside, Jake. The entire building will be gossiping if we're not careful.'

'So what?' He let go of her and followed her into the living-room before catching hold of her again. 'Coralie? No, look at me. I said, look at me.'

She hardly dared, she did not want him to see what was in her eyes. But Jake had an idea anyway, it seemed. 'You took an enormous chance with me this afternoon,' he said. 'I believe you're aware of that. There was a minute during your tirade when I could cheerfully have murdered you. To say I hated what I was hearing would be an understatement, but you were right. Worse, I think I already knew it, deep inside me. At some level, I think I'd known it all along, really, I just wouldn't face it. And you had wanted to say all that for a long time, I know. So what does all this tell me?' He asked the question confidently, pleased with the conclusion he'd reached. 'It tells me how much you care, not just about Stuart but about me, too. *Me*. Have you any idea what that means to me?'

Coralie thought she would never get the single syllable past her lips, her pulses were pounding so hard, the constriction in her throat was almost choking her. 'No.'

'Well, it means a great deal, my lovely, a very great deal.'

Expectantly she waited for more, knowing now that he really had been serious about his proposal. But there was no more. Jake simply asked her for an answer. 'So, sweetheart, what do you say? Will you give it a go?'

Give it a go? God, how defeatist that sounded! He was talking about *marriage*, and all he was asking was whether she would give it a go? Trying to form a coherent sentence at that moment was the hardest thing Coralie had ever had to do in her life. 'I don't know, Jake. I—I'm fond of you but...'

'Fond of me? Is that all?' He laughed softly, his arms forming a circle around her. She buried her face against his neck, glad of the opportunity to hide it.

'Say something, lady. I asked you a question. Is that all?'

'No,' she murmued, 'I suppose I'm very fond of you.'

Jake's low chuckle was followed immediately by an onslaught of her senses. He started kissing her as if there were no tomorrow, his lips moving from her temple to her mouth to her throat to her neck. There they lingered, because he had long since discovered she had a particularly sensitive spot, one that made her bones melt when he kissed her there.

It was impossible to think about anything, in spite of the enormity of all he had said. Coralie was aware only of Jake's nearness, of the familiar need in him, a need more urgent than it had ever been, so much so that her reaction to him was as intense as his was to her. Over and over he spoke her name softly, his hands moving to slide her gown from her shoulders. It fell to the floor and her nightie followed, shed from her body by the simple removal of the thin straps holding it in place. And then she was naked and Jake was consuming her with his eyes, his voice full of wonder, telling her how beautiful she was. 'Coralie! Oh, God, how I want you...'

Suddenly his hands and his mouth were on her breasts, making her gasp from the sheer pleasure of it. Involuntarily her head went back, her fingers lacing through the crisp black curls of his hair. 'Jake...'

He lifted her from her feet in one smooth movement, holding her high in his arms. She looked into the smouldering depths of his eyes, realising his intent: he was taking her to her bed...

'No!' It came from her quietly but sharply. Whether Jake heard her or not, she had no way of telling, because he did not stop. When they reached the door of her bedroom she started struggling in his arms, her desire for him turning insanely to resentment at all that he was taking for granted. 'Put me down. Put me down, Jake!'

He stood perfectly still, an expression of disbelief on his face. 'Coralie—for God's sake, I've asked you to marry me!'

'And that gives you the right to do with me as you will, does it? I said put me *down*.'

He put her down, but he did not let go of her. 'What's the matter with you?' he demanded. 'Look at you—you want me so much that you're trembling with it!'

She backed away from him, not bothering to deny that. Her hands were shaking as she flung on her gown. 'You're missing the point, Jake. If I were to consider marrying you——'

'Consider?' His eyes narrowed, the curiosity in that single word confirming he had indeed taken her acceptance for granted.

'Yes, consider.' Coralie held her head high, belying the torment going on inside her. 'If I do consider your proposal, there are several things we have to clear up first.'

'Namely?' He moved back into the room, draping himself negligently on the settee. 'What sort of things?'

'My work, for one.'

He shrugged. 'I wouldn't mind if you wanted to keep on working. I might be old-fashioned, but I'm not that old-fashioned.'

'There's nothing old-fashioned about you, Jacob Samuel.'

His frown was back, very much so. 'Why the ice, Coralie? Supposing you tell me what's really bothering you. You want me to wait till we're married before I make love to you, is that it? Now who's being old-fashioned?'

She wanted to hit him; his lack of sensitivity was crushing her. 'You bastard! Is that all you can think about? I'm talking about my *life*, my future, and you think I've got nothing but sex on my mind?'

Jake attempted a smile. 'Hardly.' He glanced in the direction of her bedroom, letting out an exaggerated sigh. 'More's the pity.'

It was too much for Coralie. She turned on her heel, bolted into the kitchen and slammed the door behind her, feeling so frustrated that she wanted to scream. In that moment, she wished to heaven she was not in love with this man. 'If you're not prepared to talk seriously,' she yelled in the general direction of the living-room, 'then you might just as well get out of here right now!'

Silence, a momentary silence. The door opened and Jake came in, a look of apology on his face. 'Forgive me,' he urged quietly. 'I am sorry, sweetheart. That was quite the wrong time for flippancy.'

She turned away to fill the kettle, determined he would not see the threat of tears in her eyes. 'So you are prepared to talk?'

'Of course I am.'

'Now? I mean, what about Stuart? Is Mrs Everly with him?'

'Yes, I fetched her from her cottage earlier and I explained I might be out for some time. She said she'd sleep in the bungalow tonight.'

They talked at length over several cups of coffee. There was no more flippancy from Jake, he was sitting up and taking notice, taking her seriously at last. 'So would you want to keep on working?'

'Yes, but only when I chose to, rather less than I work now, considering there would be Stuart to care for.'

'He'll be at school full-time come autumn, remember.'

'Until three-thirty or whatever, when someone will have to collect him.'

'But Mrs Everly will do that, as she does now at his playschool. It's what she's paid for.'

Coralie glanced down at her hands, uncertain as to how much she could say on the subject of Jake's housekeeper. 'I know, darling, but Mrs Everly isn't getting any younger.'

'Well, I've no intention of putting her out to pasture yet. Anyhow, that's only a detail. You could collect Stuart if you're available—and if you wanted to.'

Coralie smiled, a sad little smile. 'You should know better than that, Jake. Of course I would want to. I could work from eight till three, say, then the rest of my time would be for Stuart.'

'And me.' For just an instant he looked boyish himself, uncharacteristically uncertain of himself.

'And you,' she said quickly, covering his hand. 'And you, obviously. Which brings me to the next point, about Stuart and . . . and all that I said today. I want to make it clear that I could not stand by and watch you——'

Jake gathered her close, putting a finger to her lips. He nuzzled her hair, choosing his words carefully. 'Don't worry about that. I can't promise to change overnight, but . . . I will try to be more demonstrative with him.'

'Just show him you love him, as often as you can.'

'Unconditionally,' he said gravely, nodding against her hair. 'That was something of a revelation, the way you spoke of unconditional love.'

Again she was grateful he couldn't see her face. She closed her eyes tightly and wished desperately he could love her unconditionally, that he could love her at all . . .

'I need you,' he was saying. 'Stuart needs you and I need you, my sweet. You will remember that when you're considering my proposal?'

Coralie couldn't speak; she needed Jake, too, she could not imagine him not being in her life, but she needed to be loved as well. No. No, perhaps this was enough, this nearness, this friendship. They did have a lot going for them. But *was* it enough? He had said not a word about loving her, he had spoken only in terms of needing her.

'Coralie?'

'Yes, I heard you.'

'I've been waiting for you to ask what's in it for you.'

Her heart sank; he really had no idea of the extent of her feelings for him. He believed her to be very fond of him and no more, hence this question. 'What's in it for me?' She repeated the words lightly, keeping her face hidden, playing for time. How could she answer? 'Supposing you let me worry about that. That's all part and parcel of what I have to think about.'

She could feel him nodding, accepting what she'd said. Then she looked at him. 'I—did you have a date in mind?'

'Not really. Off the top of my head I'd say next month, say the middle of June. We could take a long honeymoon before Stuart starts school. Quite a long honeymoon,' he added with a smile.

She couldn't help laughing. 'Message received and understood, outrageous man that you are.'

Jake moved, lifting her face so he could kiss her. 'No,' he murmured, looking deep into her eyes. 'Just a man.'

A thought struck her. She straightened with a mild sense of alarm. 'What about your parents? They're in Bermuda.'

'Ever heard of aeroplanes? They'd be only too happy to fly over here, believe me.'

'What does that mean? Have they nagged you, too, about remarrying?'

'Nudged,' he amended, 'only nudged.' His arms tightened around her. It was a protective gesture and it made her heart beat faster. 'But make no mistake, little one—when I told you that if I remarried it would be wholly my own idea, I meant it. Never think for one moment that I've been bullied into this.'

'What a joke!' Coralie laughed at the notion. 'You, bullied? The person who could bully you has yet to be born.'

'Oh, I don't know about that,' he said wickedly. 'There's someone who came into this world twenty-three years ago, a female of my acquaintance, who comes very close to it at times. All of which,' he added with mock sternness, 'would have to *stop* if we were to marry.'

'Of course,' she countered, bowing her head. 'But of course, O Lord and Master.'

Jake grunted, muttering something about that being the day when pigs could fly. Little did he know, she thought, little did he know the power he really had to make her happy or unhappy, desperately unhappy. And still there was not a word of love from him. Would there ever be? Would he, could he, learn to love her in time? If she married him, wouldn't she be taking the biggest risk of her life?

That thought brought her mother to mind. 'My parents . . . Jake, you'll have to meet them. I mean, you would have to meet them.'

The frown was back. 'Of course. I'd love to, that's hardly a problem, Coralie. But what is this, I *would* have to? Does this mean you're really not going to give me an answer now, that you still want time to think?'

She eased away from him, getting to her feet because there was little else left to say at the moment, there was only the answer to this question hanging in the air. 'Yes,' she said firmly. 'Yes, I do, Jake. Give me tomorrow, all of tomorrow. I know it's Sunday but——'

'That's all right.' He got up, stretching like a panther, causing the muscles beneath his shirt to clench and tauten. 'I'll take Stuart out to lunch, just the two of us.'

Coralie moved swiftly to hug him. 'I'm very glad to hear that, darling, very glad indeed.'

'Unhand me, woman! If you don't, you'll get more than you're bargaining for . . .'

She unhanded him at once.

*   *   *

'God, you look awful!' Sophie realised she had not chosen the best moment to lean on Coralie's doorbell. 'Sorry, I can see you've only just fallen out of bed, but it's almost eleven o'clock. I know it's Sunday, but you're usually up and about by now—so what's wrong? What's that funny look in your eyes?'

'I've been up for hours, actually. I just haven't bothered to dress, that's all. What's in that carrier bag?' Coralie yawned. She had lain awake since the early hours, since Jake had left at something gone two. The morning sun had pierced the sky before she had eventually fallen asleep, only to wake again a short time later.

'It's my new outfit for the wedding.' Sophie trooped into the living-room and put the carrier bag on the table. 'I went shopping for it yesterday, remember?'

'I remember, I look forward to seeing you in it. Make us some coffee in the meantime, would you? I must pop to the bathroom.'

'Yes, madam. Then perhaps madam will tell me about this strange look in her eyes?'

Ten minutes later Sophie was standing in the middle of the room, undergoing inspection. 'What do you think?' she asked uncertainly. 'It's a bit dressy, but I thought it right for a wedding.'

'It's perfect for a wedding. You look super, both elegant and smart. Lemon suits you. I don't think I've seen you wearing that colour before.'

'I thought it was summery. We are going to have a summer this year, aren't we?'

'You can wear it twice.'

'What?' Sophie slipped out of the jacket of the costume, absently asking what Coralie was talking about.

'You'll be able to wear that wedding outfit twice.'

'Coralie! What are you saying? I don't believe this!'

The younger girl laughed, but there wasn't much mirth in it. 'Neither do I. Neither did my mother when I phoned her a while ago, neither did my father when he got on the line. It took me ages to convince them I wasn't joking.'

'They didn't approve of your getting married?'

'Approve? They were absolutely delighted, and I mean delighted. I have no wish to sound cynical, but in their eyes Jake Samuel is a very good catch—even though they haven't met him.'

'And in your eyes? Oh, really, Sophie!' She mocked herself, calling herself an idiot for saying something so unnecessary. Then she looked more closely at Coralie, seeing that the eyes in question had misted over. 'What is it?' she asked softly. 'Something is wrong. I don't understand.'

Coralie blinked back the sudden tears, she was far from unhappy, she was simply emotional. 'Oh, Sophie, I'm worried in case I'm making the biggest mistake of my life! Jake proposed to me last night, right here.' She went on to fill her friend in, needing very much to talk to someone. She had wanted to confide in her mother, but it had been impossible. Anne Dixon had responded to the news of the wedding with such euphoria, automatically and naturally assuming that Jake felt about Coralie the way Coralie felt about her husband-to-be. Shattering that illusion, that assumption, had been out of the question.

'Anyway,' she said at length, 'having talked to Jake in detail about our future, how married life would be for all of us, he was still talking only in terms of needing me. In other words, Sophie, he doesn't love me.'

'Well, at least he's been honest with you. Anyway, it's my opinion that most marriages are based on need rather than love. Oh, people usually think they're in love——'

'I haven't even got that much, though. Jake doesn't love me, he doesn't even think himself in love with me—and even there, there is a difference, don't you think?'

'I don't think, I know. The *ideal* is to love and to stay in love, too. But that—well, personally I've given up on fairy-tales. I'm no dreamer.'

Coralie's head came up, it was as if those words were meant to trigger her. They had come innocently from Sophie, but... 'But I am. At least, that's what Jake is always telling me.'

'Maybe. You're not a fool, however. You must have weighed up the pros and cons of marrying him.'

There was a wry smile on Coralie's mouth. 'You could say that—I spent most of the night doing it. And,' she added, able to smile fully, 'the pros far outweigh the cons. You see, I need Jake, too, quite apart from the fact that I love him. I'm—I'm just hoping that my loving him will be enough for us both, enough to make a success of it.'

'But you have definitely made up your mind? You will go through with it?'

Go through with it. Why did that make it sound like an ordeal? She nodded, in spite of everything she was going to marry Jake, she had known it since the moment he'd asked her, really. 'Yes.'

Sophie leaned over to plant a kiss on her cheek. 'Then I'll wish you all the luck in the world. So, when's the big day?'

'Some time next month.'

'So soon? What did your parents have to say about that?'

'Dad grunted and my mother squealed. She's convinced she can't possibly find anything to wear in so short a time.'

'I know the feeling. Will you be married from home?'

'No, I——' Coralie stopped abruptly. 'Do you know, that's one thing Jake and I didn't talk about. I just took it for granted we'd get married here in Salisbury.'

'Play your cards right,' Sophie quipped, 'and they might let you have the cathedral for the occasion.'

'Cut it out, Sophie. If I have my way, which I will, it'll be in a register office. In the circumstances, I don't want churches and vows and all that.'

'Wouldn't that disappoint your mother?'

'It did a bit, when I mentioned it, but she'll adjust to the idea. What I didn't tell her was that I'll probably get married down here. But it seems sensible. There's Jake's sister and her family, his parents flying out from Bermuda—and there's Stuart to consider. I think it would be better all round.'

'Then you'll have to sort it out with the fortunate Mr Samuel, and the sooner the better,' Sophie suggested. 'Is he coming over today?'

'No, he's taking Stuart to——' Again Coralie stopped, looking at Sophie with an expression of horror on her face.

'What now? What's the matter?'

'Jake, I forgot to ring him. I haven't told him yet. I mean, I haven't told him I'm going to marry him.'

Sophie looked heavenward. 'You mean you've told your parents, but you haven't told the man concerned? I think I've heard everything now!'

'Well, I did tell him I'd need all day today to think about it.'

'Yes, dear, but any normal girl would let her man be the first to hear that his fate has been sealed. You might well laugh, Coralie. Look, I'm going. For goodness' sake, since you have made up your mind, ring the man and put him out of his suspense!'

She did so the moment the door closed behind Sophie. 'Jake? How come you're answering the phone?'

'It's Sunday, remember? Mrs Everly's day off. She's gone out for the day.'

'Oh. Yes. Well, I didn't sleep too well last night. I'm a bit dopey.'

'So, what else is new?' There was a sudden silence at Jake's end. When next he spoke, all pretence at humour was gone. 'You had a lot on your mind. I...didn't expect to hear from you this early. Did you reach a conclusion? Do you want me to come over?'

'No. I mean yes. Sorry, what I really mean——'

'For heaven's sake, just say it!' He almost shouted at her. 'I can't hold my breath much longer, Coralie.'

So he cared to some extent, if the tension in his voice was anything to go by. 'No, I don't want you to come over. You've planned to take Stuart out to lunch and I wouldn't change that for all the coal in Newcastle.'

'Tea in China, if you must talk in clichés. You mean all the tea in China, you wretched girl——'

'I know what I mean,' she said haughtily, knowing also how badly she was behaving in prolonging his suspense. 'I always know what I mean. Now, where were we?'

'Oh, there was just this little matter of a proposal of marriage...'

'Oh, yes.'

'Yes? As in *yes*?'

She relented, unable to tease him, or herself, any longer. 'As in, yes, I accept, Jake. So we have to talk again, tonight preferably. Can you come over as soon as Mrs Everly gets back?'

'Why don't you come here? You can break the glad tidings to her yourself then. I have a feeling she won't mind in the least.'

Doubts crossed Coralie's mind again. Glad tidings, that was all, that was how Jake regarded the news of her acceptance. There was no euphoria in his voice. His housekeeper would probably respond with more enthusiasm than he was showing. 'I have that feeling, too, but I'd rather you came here so we can be sure of no interruptions.'

Jake's humour was back, his deep voice was velvety smooth when he asked her what she had in mind.

'A *discussion*, Jake. That's all. We've got a heck of a lot of sorting out to do.'

A few weeks later all the sorting out had been done. A few weeks and probably a hundred telephone calls. Jake had called his parents first, then he'd spoken to his sister and brother-in-law, and on it had gone. But, before he spoke to anyone at all about his plans, he sat his son on his knee and informed him gently that he was going to have a new mother.

When Coralie expressed her preference for a register office wedding, Jake did not demur. He, too, had assumed they would marry in the south, given that his house could accommodate several people for the weekend. The date was set for the third Saturday in June, and time was flying. After the invitations had been sent out, flowers ordered, a photographer booked, Jake reserved a private room at the Red Lion Hotel for the reception. They had whittled the guest list down to one hundred, and the management at the Red Lion was delighted to offer a wide range of menus. Because Coralie expressed a preference for a buffet reception, that was what she would have, Jake said.

He wrote her an outrageously generous cheque for her wedding outfit and for what he called 'the other bits a new bride needs'. She could not have asked more, not at a practical level at least, of the man she was going to marry. He was efficient, considerate and consistently deferential to her. There was only one point on which he would not compromise: he wanted a month-long honeymoon, in fact he had already arranged it.

'But, Jake, we can't expect Mrs Everly to look after Stuart single-handedly for four weeks. It isn't fair——'

'She wouldn't mind in the least. She's working her notice, anyway.' His housekeeper, joyous at the news of the forthcoming wedding, had finally been able to tell her employer of her own wants. Jake had been very surprised by her wanting to leave; he had been openly disappointed, too, but all he had asked was her agreement to stay on until he got back from his honeymoon, to look after things and give him and Coralie a chance to find a replacement.

'I know she wouldn't mind,' Coralie said, 'but that isn't the point. I feel we'd be taking liberties if——'

'Will you let me finish, madam? She'll only be taking care of Stuart for two weeks. During the first two weeks we're away, she'll be down in Bournemouth with her sister, organising her own new life. I discussed things with her this morning, so there!' He caught Coralie to him and started nibbling her neck. This, in full view of

Stuart who was sprawled on the living-room floor with crayons and a colouring-book.

The child turned round to watch the display, an attitude of boredom in his voice. 'You two are always kissing! Why don't you tell Coralie, Daddy?'

'Tell me what, poppet?' She shook Jake off; it was getting difficult to keep him from constantly manhandling her. Not that she could blame him; they'd barely had a moment's peace since the wedding date had been set, they'd had hardly any time alone together. And tomorrow his parents were arriving, well in advance of the wedding, by their own choice. That they wanted to get to know their future daughter-in-law was not helping, either, as far as Coralie's pre-wedding nerves were concerned.

The previous weekend had been racked with tension. She had driven with Jake to her home in Yorkshire, wound up like a spring, anticipating her parents' reaction to him. They had not taken Stuart along; she had felt it would be too much on this initial meeting, that it would be difficult to cope with as it was. Her greatest fear had been that her mother, if not her father, would realise instinctively that all was not as it should be, that her future husband was not in love with her.

As it turned out, her fears had been unfounded. Jake had been sufficiently attentive to mask the truth of the situation and, if either of her parents had suspected something was wrong, they had given no hint of their suspicions.

Her latest worry was unfounded, too, it turned out. Stuart was now explaining that he was going to stay with his grandma and grandpa. 'In Bermuda. They're going to take me home with them while you and Daddy go on your honey...honeything. What do you call it?'

'Honeymoon.' It was a chorus. 'So,' Jake went on, 'Mrs Everly will only have to cope for two weeks with Stuart, as will my parents. They're getting on in years, and having Stuart for a month-long stretch would be too much for them, too, much as they love him.'

'Well!' Coralie smiled, relieved. 'I'm impressed with your organising abilities yet again, Jake. But who'll bring Stuart back from Bermuda?'

'Friends of my parents, neighbours of theirs who are coming to London for a silver wedding anniversary. So it's all worked out beautifully, hasn't it? Our minds can be at rest while we're on our honeything.'

Coralie laughed again, asking him yet again where that was going to be; all she knew so far was that she would need a passport and lightweight, summer clothing. Yet again Jake refused point-blank to tell her. It was, he said, his business, not hers.

'Humph! I should be in on this, Jake. After all, I am going to be there!' she said, coaxing him, trailing her fingers down his back. 'So, what are your plans? Come on, tell me!'

He leaned close, very close, moving his lips tantalisingly against her ear. He whispered of his plans for her—but these had nothing to do with the destination of their honeymoon.

'Coralie?' Stuart got to his feet, came over and tugged at her skirt. 'Where's my new racing car? And why is your face all red?'

'Is it really?' She tossed her hair back, blowing at it from the corner of her mouth. 'Come here and give me a cuddle, Stuart.' Over the top of his head she looked at Jake, her blush deepening even further.

'Do you want a cuddle, too, Daddy?' It was still there, the hesitation in the child, the uncertainty that his father might not be in the mood for cuddling. But it was starting to happen, and Jake was very much aware that time was all that was needed.

'I certainly do!' He held his arms wide, enfolding his eager son firmly when the boy flung himself into his embrace.

When Jake's eyes met with hers again, Coralie had to look away. The scene was so poignant, more satisfying than words could convey. But Jake's eyes had just spoken only of his gratitude to her.

Gratitude, and admiration, perhaps. But nothing else.

CHAPTER EIGHT

CORALIE stepped out of the register office into brilliant sunshine, her arm linked with that of her husband. Patiently they posed again for the photographer, as they would yet again during their reception. Their wedding had gone beautifully; she had been so nervous, she thought she would never get through the ceremony, simple though it had been, without making a mess of it.

As Jake bent to kiss her, much to the delight of all who were watching and clicking their own cameras, she felt a stab of regret that they had not married in church. The twinkle of the diamond on her left hand, snuggled close against her brand new wedding ring, also evoked a pang of regret. Jake's generosity with her engagement ring had been breathtaking... but it had been an unconventional engagement in her eyes, lacking the necessary ingredient of love. On his part. She could have stood proudly in church, taking this man to be her husband with all the vows that went with a religious ceremony, but she had dismissed the idea from the beginning because it would have been a sham, obliging Jake to say things he could not mean.

So here she was, legally married to him and loving him so much that it almost hurt. She thought about the weeks ahead with a mixture of trepidation and excitement—and nervousness. In a few hours' time they would leave the reception, leave Salisbury for London. They were staying there overnight, at the Dorchester, and in the morning they were flying from Heathrow to a destination still unknown to her.

For the moment Coralie was unconcerned about that. She was concerned about tonight, tonight when she would be in Jake's arms and there would be no holding back. Again she knew a pang of regret, for a different reason. Although they had not in fact been remotely close to making love since the night Jake had proposed, he had asked her, the following evening, to be 'on the safe side' and get the Pill: Coralie had agreed simply with a nod of her head; there had been no discussion. There had been no need for a discussion; she had absorbed the information implicit in his request, and had herself thought it sensible to take the best precaution available. To think in terms of their having children would be going too far. Their marriage might not last. She knew it and he knew it, too.

'Coralie?' He was smiling down at her now. 'Come on, the car awaits us. You have a wedding reception to attend, remember?'

He reached out to adjust the hat she was wearing—a plain, broad-brimmed picture hat, impossibly white, which she would never wear again. She disliked hats; this one had been her mother's idea, when she had arrived in Salisbury earlier in the week she had insisted that Coralie should wear a hat on her wedding day. Coralie had obliged only to please her. The dress she was wearing was silk, also plain and gleaming white. Well, at least she would be able to wear the dress again.

'Gorgeous!' Jake was saying. 'You look adorable in that hat.' She pulled a face at him and he laughed, taking her hand as they walked to the waiting car. 'I hope someone got a snap of that funny face, it would serve you right.'

She barely heard him. She glanced along the line of cars, feeling disorientated. Mrs Jacob Samuel, she really was Mrs Samuel now, married to a man who had proposed quite simply because he needed her in his life. Well, he had her. But what of the future? What would it bring?

'It's too late for second thoughts.' Jake's voice brought her head round quickly; they were in the car and she had been staring out of the window, still dazed.

'I wasn't having second thoughts,' she lied. 'I was thinking how fortunate I am, we are. You get on beautifully with my parents and—well, your mother and father are delightful.' So they were; they were both in their seventies, warm-hearted and very wise, particularly Jake's father. There was a wisdom in him which did not necessarily come with age and, if there was one person who knew that all was not as it should be between Coralie and Jake, it was Godfrey Samuel.

'The feeling is mutual,' Jake said, reaching for her hand and squeezing it. 'They think you're delightful, too. If they've told me once, they've told me a dozen times how lucky I am to land a girl like you.'

She couldn't help laughing. 'That makes me sound like a fish! That was your phrase, not theirs. Your father would be more apt to say something like, "to *win* a girl like Coralie", darling man that he is.'

Her husband's brows went slowly upwards, his deep blue eyes gleaming with pleasure and amusement. 'You've certainly got old Godfrey weighed up accurately! Come here, come closer, it's been too long since I kissed you.'

They were still kissing when the car stopped and the driver was opening the door for them.

*   *   *

'Coralie? How are you doing? Oh, Mrs Dixon, your husband wants a word with you, he asked me to tell you.'

Anne excused herself when Sophie came in, leaving her daughter to finish changing in the room provided by the hotel. Coralie looked worriedly at her friend and shrugged. 'I've drunk too much champagne, which was stupid of me.'

'No, it wasn't. This is your wedding day, you're entitled. Anyhow, it doesn't seem to have helped much,' she added shrewdly, eyeing the younger girl closely. 'You're as nervous now as you were in your flat this morning.'

'Of course I am!' Coralie snapped. 'Because I'm scared, that's why. I'm riddled with negative thoughts.' The day had been perfect in every way, the reception had been full of laughter and music and a happy, party atmosphere, yet she could not shake off her worries, in spite of the champagne she had drunk. 'You know Jake wants me to put my flat on the market as soon as we get back from our honeymoon. And what could I say? I wanted to say no, let's see how things go before I give up my home, but how could I say that?'

'You couldn't,' Sophie agreed. 'Look, love, try to see the positive side of things. When Jake asked you to marry him, you spent the night weighing up the situation—and you accepted that you both had a great deal going for you. So give yourself a chance. You and Jake are friends, at least, and you're good for each other. You've changed a lot since you first met him, you know, and I'm talking about positive changes. As for him, well, at least ten people have remarked to me this afternoon about the changes you've brought about in Jake. I was in no position to judge—but his sister has been raving on about the wonders you've worked with him. She said it's a pleasure to see him laugh so easily these days, she said it's as if you've thrown a switch inside him and made him come alive again. So think about that, Coralie, because if Jake doesn't love you, he certainly must be heading in that direction, at least.'

'Oh, Sophie, thank you! Thank you for saying that, all of it.' She put her arms around her friend's neck and hugged her, blinking back tears at the same time. 'You've made me feel so much better!'

'Good. Now, come on, you must get a move on. Jake's all ready out there, waiting for you.'

An hour later the newlyweds had managed to get away, extracting themselves amid a torrent of smiles and tears, well-wishing and the inevitable teasing. They were being driven to London in a hired limousine; Jake had said there was no point in leaving his car at the airport for a month. He was looking at her now with concern, asking her what was wrong, but she couldn't tell him what was on her mind. The last person she had looked at as they'd driven away was Mrs Everly, waving frantically and dabbing at her eyes with a hankie. It had not been difficult to guess what the woman was thinking, what she simply must have been reminded of. She must have been thinking back ten years, to the time when she had first started working for Jake. Jake and his new wife, just back from their honeymoon...the idea of that was preying on Coralie's mind, unnecessarily reminding her how different the circumstances were for Jake now, how different this honeymoon was going to be, with a wife he didn't love.

'It's nothing, Jake. I'm just exhausted.'

He nodded, understanding. 'Today was a hell of a strain, wasn't it? If it's any consolation, I feel the same.'

She glanced at him quickly, wondering to what extent he shared her feelings, her doubts. For all she knew, he might be regretting what he'd done; the strain could have been twice as bad for him. She turned to look out of the window, shaking herself mentally, knowing that she must not, dare not, continue to think in such terms. As Sophie had said, she had to give herself a chance, she had to give herself and Jake a chance, and reading ominous implications into his words was hardly the way to do that.

But it didn't work. The effect of Sophie's pep talk, of her own resolutions, was very short-lived. Knowing what she had to do, knowing the sensible thing to do, did not help her actually to do it. On the contrary, she grew more and more uptight as the hours progressed, finding herself unable to behave in a manner opposite to what she was really feeling. She did try—time and again she reminded herself to smile, to put on a bright face and make an effort—but she could not fool herself and she could not fool Jake, either.

'What is it, Coralie? And don't tell me again that you're exhausted. It's more than that. I'd like the truth this time.'

It was almost nine o'clock and they were just finishing a superb meal in their suite at the Dorchester. Again everything was perfect, the attentive service they were getting, the beautifully furnished rooms and the food itself. Coralie had only picked at her dinner; she had been more interested in the champagne that had come with it, compliments of the management. She reached for the bottle, seeing with some dismay that there was only one glassful left in it.

'That won't help.' Jake's hand covered hers, lifting it from the neck of the bottle. 'That won't solve anything,

Coralie. Drinking never does that, never makes your problems go away.'

'Problems?' She flashed him a smile, it was an effort but she had to keep trying. 'I haven't got any problems, Jake!'

He responded to that with a gentle smile, a slight shake of his head which made her feel guilty. He had done so much to make this day special, perfect, and he was looking at her now with unconcealed disappointment. 'It's time to talk, Coralie. It's time you told me what's on your mind. If you are having second thoughts about marrying me, please say so.'

'No!' It came too forcefully, too loudly, and yet it was the truth. It wasn't that she was having second thoughts, exactly, it was just that she was afraid, afraid of many things. But how could she tell him that? He would think her crazy if he knew the half of what was going through her mind. Worse, he would probably laugh his head off if he had any idea that the image of the big bed in the next room kept haunting her. That was part of her problem, possibly the major part, because the prospect of getting into bed with Jake had become dreadful to her. It was, she knew, just too ridiculous, given how much she wanted him, given that she had ached for him earlier in the day when he had been kissing her on the way to the reception.

'Then tell me what it is,' he said softly. 'If something is wrong, give me the chance to put it right, sweetheart.' When she said nothing, he added, 'Supposing you tell me what's going through your mind right now?'

She tried to. This was a dangerous moment, she knew that, an important moment which could either resolve or worsen her situation. If she didn't make at least an attempt to be honest with him, he might withdraw. On the other hand, if she were honest with him, he might get angry. 'I feel . . . sort of trapped.'

'Trapped?' Jake picked up her left hand, his thumb and forefinger closing around her wedding ring. 'Trapped by this?'

Coralie felt like crying. She wouldn't, she dared not, but she wanted to. 'No. Not by that, Jake.'

He looked at her carefully, his eyes examining hers to determine whether she had told the truth. 'OK,' he said simply, astonishing her by letting the matter drop. 'How about a cup of coffee and some dessert?'

'I—nothing else to eat for me, thanks. But I'd love some coffee.'

He crossed the room to pick up the telephone and talk to room service. Little was said in the time it took for them to deliver the coffee and remove the table on which their dinner had arrived. Jake made a couple of remarks about the décor and the furnishings, and Coralie responded with genuine enthusiasm. Their suite was luxurious in the extreme, and she was delighted with it. She just wished it contained two beds instead of one, she just wished she could behave like a normal woman and stop this mad carousel of thoughts spinning in her mind. Why in God's name was she privately blaming Jake for wanting her? Why was she convincing herself that, in the absence of love, it was lust that was responsible for his marrying her? Why was she accusing him of motives which were in no way a part of his character? It made no sense, none at all, but there it was.

'I'm going out for a walk.'

'You—*what*?' She could not believe she had heard Jake correctly. He had just drained his coffee-cup and, when she asked him whether he would like a refill, this was his response. 'What did you say, Jake?'

'I said I'm going out for a walk.' He was already on his feet, shrugging and smiling. 'I need some air, I need to walk off that huge meal, OK?'

'OK,' she said, not knowing what else to say. Unlike her, he had eaten heartily. Unlike her, he seemed not to have a care in the world. 'Am I invited to come with you?'

'No,' he said simply. He bent to kiss her on the forehead, ruffling her hair as though she were a child. 'You can do your own thing for an hour or two.'

'An hour or two?' She couldn't believe this, she could not believe that on this, her wedding night, she was to be left alone for an *hour or two*! She was staring at him but he didn't know it, he was already opening the outer door of their suite.

He turned and gave her a wave. 'See you later—but don't wait up for me.'

Then he was gone, leaving her to stare after him in utter bewilderment. It wasn't that she minded his going out, she simply could not believe that he had!

Minutes passed, how many she had no idea, before she shifted herself. She placed the coffee-tray outside the door and then she ran a bath. It was bliss, so much so that she almost fell asleep in it. When she emerged, the radio alarm-clock on the side of the bed told her it was ten-thirty. There was no sign of her husband. So what the hell was she supposed to do with herself? Spend the first night of her honeymoon watching television? Alone, at that!

It was precisely what she did. She got into bed and flicked the remote-control switch that brought the screen alive. But she didn't register anything, all she could think about was Jake, roaming around the West End of London while she sat prettily in bed, dressed in the long,

black scrap of a nightie given to her by Sophie as part
of a wedding present.

'This is for you,' Sophie had said, handing her a small,
gift-wrapped package one day when they were alone in
her flat. 'Though I suppose it's a present for Jake, too,
in a way. You'll see what I mean when you open it!' She
had added the last words with a wink. And Coralie had
seen. The nightdress was pure silk, featherlight and soft
and spelling seduction.

At eleven o'clock she turned the TV off and looked
down at herself, not knowing whether to laugh at her
situation, cry about it or be angry over it. There was
still no sign of Jake. At eleven-thirty, when still he hadn't
returned, she wondered if there was cause for worry. She
dismissed the idea, telling herself that Jake Samuel was
more than capable of looking after himself.

Which meant there was nothing for her to do but go
to sleep.

It was a quarter past midnight when Jake came back.
Coralie had been sleeping, but it must have been a light
sleep because his movements in the bathroom woke her.
She opened her eyes, registered the time, registered her
relief at knowing he was all right, and closed them again.
She felt half drugged, she was very tired both physically
and mentally. The champagne which had earlier failed
to change her mood was working now, inducing a
physical relaxation she could not have shaken off if she
had wanted to.

It was Jake who did that. He emerged from their en-
suite bathroom, flicked off the lights and crossed the
room in the dark. Without a word he slipped into bed
beside her, and at once her brain sprang into action. Of
its own accord her body seemed to shed its lethargy,
tensing suddenly as though it had a mind of its own,

quite independent of her. She kept her eyes closed, anticipating, waiting for Jake to reach for her.

But he did not reach for her. He made himself comfortable, and merely covered her hand with his beneath the bedclothes. After a moment of unbearable silence and stillness, she said quietly, 'I'm not asleep, Jake.'

There came only a murmur from him before he turned his back to her. 'Mmm?' He wasn't touching her at all now; it felt as though he was miles away. 'Settle down, my lovely, tomorrow will be another long day.'

She smiled into the darkness. 'Why? Where are we going?'

'Paradise Beach,' he muttered. 'If you must know.'

'What? Where's that? Jake?' The moonlight filtering through the curtains was enough for her see the outline of his back. She was fixed on the sight, hardly able to credit that he was actually falling asleep on her. 'Jake, answer me!'

He turned around slowly and flung an arm across her waist. 'In the Caribbean.'

Coralie moved closer, registering the fresh scent of toothpaste on his breath, beyond which was the faintest hint that he had drunk some brandy. She also realised he was not wearing a stitch...and that her heart was thumping like a mad thing. They were going to the Caribbean? For a whole month? Excitement gripped her, she reached out to touch his shoulder. 'Where in the Caribbean?'

Jake didn't answer, he gathered her close against him, nuzzling her hair, letting the fingers of one hand trail along the soft silk of her nightdress. 'Mmm, you feel so good, little dreamer, you smell good, too...'

'Jake Samuel,' she said with a warning in her voice, 'will you please stop teasing me? *Where* are we going, exactly?'

His laughter was low and soft against her ear. 'To the Paradise Beach hotel, Paradise Beach, Barbados. Are you satisfied now? Will you go to sleep now?'

Silently she laughed and cursed him at the same time. She took his face between her hands and kissed him hungrily on the mouth, inching closer so the entire length of her body was pressed against his. But Jake had already responded to her; she had aroused him as he had already aroused her, his body made that perfectly obvious. She moved her lips to his cheek and to his throat, talking to him between kisses. 'To sleep, Jake? Is that really what you want me to do?' Very lightly she nibbled his shoulder, urging him even closer when she slid an arm around his back, letting her fingers explore the hard contour of the muscles there. She wanted to explore every inch of him, to discover everything there was to know about his body. 'You're quite sure,' she whispered, 'that you want me to stop what I'm doing and go to sleep?'

'I'm—oh, God, Coralie!' Suddenly she was on her back, he was calling her a seductress and turning her in his arms. She had only a moment in which to laugh, in which to realise how cleverly *he* had been seducing her from the moment he had left her alone earlier—and oh, how she loved him for that! He had known all along of her nervousness, of her self-consciousness.

And then there was no more thought. Jake's kiss blotted out everything but her need. Beneath the delicious onslaught of his mouth she moved almost desperately against him. Her body wanted to know the full weight of his, she wanted him wholly on top of her, she wanted him inside her, now! This was not enough, the erotic probing of his tongue, the caress of his hands on her breasts was not enough. She spoke his name on a gasp, urging him to possess her. 'Jake, please...please!'

But Jake was a long way from making love to her fully, a very long way; although his hands were trembling when he slipped her nightdress from her shoulders, he was in no hurry to take her. With infinite tenderness he laid a trail of gossamer kisses from her lips to her throat, evoking the response she never failed to give when he touched that particularly sensitive spot. Coralie let her eyes close, hardly noticing that Jake had reached out to switch on a lamp. She was naked in his arms now and totally without inhibition, abandoning herself to his caresses with joy and with a passion she had not known she was capable of.

Beneath the touch of his hand her thighs parted in a complete offering of herself, a willing offering of that most intimate part of her. A shudder of pure ecstasy ran through her as he touched her very lightly, gently, easily coaxing her into a frenzy of yearning, a yearning she felt sure she could no longer bear. 'Jake—oh, Jake, I want you so much! Now. Please!'

'Sssh.' His lips were against her breast, teasing the erect tip of it, nibbling and sucking, driving her deeper into a whirling spiral of desire. She was cradled firmly in his left arm, held in such a way that he could do with her as he wished, and when his mouth moved back to hers he found her lips already parted. He kissed her briefly and lightly, teasing her further by this withholding, murmuring words of encouragement she could barely respond to. Her breathing was ragged and fast, all her awareness was centred now on the yawning ache inside her, on the play of his fingers at that most delicate part of her.

'Jake...'

'Yes, my lovely. Soon, soon, I promise. Come on, my darling, show me——'

Coralie heard no more. A cry tore from her, blotting out his crooning words as her entire body went into a sweet spasm of release that went on and on. And still he was talking softly to her, encouraging her and praising her, even as she relaxed, spent, in his arms. 'There's a lovely girl, my good and gorgeous girl.' He was kissing her closed eyelids now, speaking with a smile in his voice.

She leaned her head against his chest and marvelled at his self-control, at the patience he had shown with her. In that moment it never occurred to her to try to hold back what she wanted to tell him, needed to tell him. 'Jake, I love you, I love you so much...'

He smiled at her, saying nothing further. Her forehead was moist with perspiration, and he gently brushed her hair from it before kissing her once more on the mouth.

Coralie looked into his eyes questioningly, unsure of herself. Jake's body was rigid with tension while she— she had nothing more to give. 'Darling? I don't under-stand——'

'Sssh, it's all right.' He smiled, blocking her words with his lips. He reached for her hand and guided it to his body, and then she understood. She didn't believe it, but she understood. She did have more to give; it was happening all over again, again she was feeling that deep stirring of desire, again it was Jake who took control, but it was she who was making love to him now.

If there had been any possibility of her inhibition, her nervousness reasserting itself, that possibility vanished in those moments. Jake knew precisely how it was with her. When next she cried out for him to possess her, he did, but not before he had reassured her once more. 'Trust me,' he whispered. 'I won't hurt you, Coralie.'

Nor did he; she was so open to him there was little chance of that. She knew only a fleeting, concentrated ache as Jake moved slowly into her, easing the path no other man had taken, and after that there was nothing but the most incredible pleasure. Boldly she put her hands on his hips, encouraging him now, urging him deeper inside her with the thrusting of her own body. She looked up at him with eyes full of wonder, revelling in these first moments of joining with him, of being one with him. He smiled at her, a smile unlike any she had seen from him before, his deep blue eyes locked with hers in the most private and intimate celebration.

CHAPTER NINE

THE RHYTHM of their lovemaking accelerated. Outside their room in the Paradise Beach hotel the sun was shining in all its glory, the sea was lapping gently on to the white beach and, dimly, there was the sound of someone laughing.

Coralie was aware of none of it; for three days and three nights she and Jake had spent much of their time in bed, locked in each other's arms, their bodies entwined together as they were now. 'Jake . . .' She unlaced the fingers she had locked around his neck, moving her hands so they were on either side of his face. She didn't need to ask, he was already kissing her as she wanted to be kissed, completing their total embrace with mouth on mouth, heart on heart—until she broke it by gasping, throwing her head back, speaking his name over and over.

Everything intensified again. Jake took his weight on one elbow and reached for her hip with his other hand, shifting her position slightly as he thrust into her faster, deeper, until at last she was crying out in an ecstasy of release. Simultaneously they climaxed, relaxing heavily against each other when it was over, as they always did, arms holding, cheek against cheek.

It was Jake who spoke first, some time later. He had drifted into a brief sleep but Coralie had not, she had lain still, her body relaxed totally, still humming with the aftermath of their lovemaking. As always during these moments she felt so good, so alive, but sometimes unwelcome thoughts would sneak in to spoil her stillness. It was happening now and she was helpless to prevent it. She was wondering for the hundredth time whether Jake had actually heard what she had told him on their wedding night, or whether in the throes of passion her words had not registered with him. He had never referred to her admission of loving him, never alluded to it in any way at all. Given the state he was in at the time, he might well have not heard her. She simply didn't know.

'Coralie?'

She closed her eyes, having a good idea what he was about to say. That was another thing, Jake was concerned to the point of fanaticism about her taking care with contraception. He asked her daily if she had remembered to take her Pill, and usually he did so after lovemaking, as if he needed reassurance that he was not going to be trapped by an unwanted pregnancy. She tried not to resent this, telling herself it was perfectly reasonable, that he was entitled to his opinions and feelings—but he had never asked her how she felt about this, he had never asked her whether she might like to have a child, sooner or later. It was that that hurt, his treating the whole thing as if he were the only person concerned.

'I'm going to do some serious sunbathing this afternoon,' she said at length. 'How about you?' She turned to look at him, wondering whether he would join her or whether he would take off yet again on one of his solitary walks. In the three days they had been here he had done that three times. It was as though he needed some part of the day to himself, if only an hour, and it was something else Coralie had had to think about, telling herself it was perfectly reasonable for her husband to need his own space.

'It sounds good to me,' he said, surprising her.

They spent the whole afternoon sunbathing, opting for the beach rather than the loungers by the hotel swimming pool. They both preferred to swim in the sea, it was so gorgeous, so blue and clean, sparkling brilliantly under the sun. Paradise Beach was perfect for a honeymoon, perfect for anyone who was pleased by the simple things in life.

As the days passed they did other simple things together: walking and riding along the sands at sunset. Sometimes they would play tennis before dinner, working up an appetite for the different kinds of food it had taken several days to adjust to. Coralie was not adventurous when it came to trying new foods, but Jake was. She was still learning about the man she had married, still discovering what did and did not make him tick. He loved to dance in the conventional fashion, he loved to listen to the Caribbean music, but he did not care at all for disco music and what he referred to as 'gyrating wildly under lights that give you a headache'.

They went into Bridgetown often, to Trafalgar Square—a name which amused Coralie—and the bustling waterfront. They strolled around the duty-free shops and bought bits and bobs they would probably never use, and presents with a difference for Stuart. Coralie was missing Stuart and, if she were honest, could hardly wait to see him again, even though she was enjoying herself enormously in Barbados. By the end of the third week she was feeling she had had enough, but she would not risk hurting Jake's feelings by saying so. He was missing Stuart too, he said as much, but he was also loving every minute of his holiday.

No, not every minute. That was an exaggeration. He was loving *almost* every minute, perhaps, but there were odd times when he grew very quiet, engrossed in his own thoughts, and this was always a sign to Coralie that he was about to take off and be on his own for a while. Only once did she ask him about it, lightly and casually, one evening when she emerged from the shower to find him sitting on their balcony, staring out across the Caribbean. There was a strange look in his eyes, and he didn't even hear her approach him.

'Jake? What is it? What's the matter?'

Startled, he turned to face her, looking at her in such a way that he seemed not to recognise her for a moment. 'I was thinking.'

'I gathered that!' She laughed and sat next to him, pulling her towelling dressing-gown more closely around her. 'But what about?'

It was seconds before he answered, and when he did so his eyes were on the sea again. 'Life. The past. The future.'

'What about them?'

'For God's sake!' he snapped. 'We might be married, Coralie, but that does not mean I have to share my every thought with you! I'm entitled to some privacy, aren't I?' With that, he got up and stalked away from her. The next thing she heard was the slamming of their bedroom door as he left.

Stunned, she sat for long minutes with tears in her eyes, staring at the water unseeingly. There had been no call for that, none at all. He had been unfair; she had not been prying, she had merely worried that *he* was worried about something. She hadn't wanted to impinge on his privacy, she took pains not to do that, she had only wanted to... to help if she could. Something was bothering him, it had from the beginning of their time here, and the fact that he would not share it with her made her feel insecure all over again.

She let her eyes close, acknowledging how true it was that one never really knew a person until one lived with that person. Or was she getting paranoid? Was her own insecurity making her read more into things than really existed? No. There was about Jake a certain holding back, a reserve she simply could not penetrate. Nor would she try to, not any more. If he felt so strongly about not having his privacy invaded, she would never attempt to do it again.

Things would be different, she told herself, when they got home, when they established a life-style together on a day-to-day basis, one which included Stuart. This honeymoon was not a real example of how things would be, it was not a typical indication of their future life together, she must remember that. Their future life. What had Jake been thinking of the future? What had he been thinking of the past, his past? He must have been thinking about his wife, mustn't he? Inevitably this, his second honeymoon, must be reminding him of his first, with Alison, the wife he had loved and lost . . .

Oh, God! Was he still in love with Alison? Was that it?

At the start of their fourth and last week in Barbados, Coralie did get some indication of Jake's thoughts about the future, the immediate future at least. They were in the hotel coffee-shop, having a mid-afternoon snack, when he told her he'd been thinking they should re-do the bungalow, that they should redecorate several rooms and change the furniture in the living-room.

'What do you think?' he asked. 'Would you want to take it on yourself or do you think it would be too much? Shall we get someone in to do it?'

'Certainly not!' She laughed, giving him an exaggerated look of indignation. 'I'm more than capable, and besides, I want to do it.'

'I know you're capable, my lovely, but are you sure it won't be too much? Not that there's any hurry, of course.'

'Exactly. I can do it as the mood takes me. I'll look forward to it.'

Seeming satisfied, Jake nodded. 'And that reminds me, the first thing we must do when we get back is to put your flat up for sale.'

For a minute she did not respond, her mind was racing furiously. She was wondering how she could postpone this from happening—without rocking the boat as far as Jake was concerned. 'Well,' she said casually, 'there's no particular hurry about that, either, Jake. I mean, it isn't as if we're desperate for the money.'

'No, of course not. But what's the point in delaying? What exactly do you have in mind, Coralie?'

'I just thought we could leave it for a while, that's all. After all, my flat is the first home I've ever had of my own and——'

'And you don't want to give it up, is that what you're saying?'

'Not exactly,' she hedged, glancing round to make sure they were not being overheard. If they were, it would strike even the most uninterested of eavesdroppers as being a peculiar conversation between man and wife. 'I just thought . . . well, that it might be sensible to see how things go with us, in the circumstances?'

'Circumstances?' Jake said too loudly. 'What circumstances?'

Again Coralie glanced around. 'I don't think this is the time and place for this kind of discussion, Jake.'

He ignored that. 'What circumstances?' he demanded angrily. 'What the hell is that supposed to mean?'

Her heart sank. More than anything in the world, she wished she could tell him what was on her mind. She wished she could point out how insecure she felt, how she hated it when he closed off from her, how he had never, ever spoken one word of love to her. Oh, he spoke possessively often enough, she was always 'his lovely' or 'his little dreamer', but that was all. And she was beginning to understand why, too. In spite of what he'd said about being over Alison's death, as time went on she had realised he was not over it. Maybe he thought he was, he probably did believe he was, but it was not the case.

'Nothing,' she said. 'It doesn't mean anything, Jake.' She could almost see herself squirming, wishing she had kept her mouth shut as far as the sale of her flat was concerned.

'Don't give me that. I'll tell you what it means; it means you might have made a legal commitment to me, but you're not thinking in terms of permanence. It means our marriage is on trial as far as you're concerned, or I'm on trial——'

'Jake, that's ridiculous!'

'Well, what else am I supposed to think? What else am I supposed to make of the fact that you want to keep your flat on? You want it as a bolt-hole, somewhere you can run to when you've had enough of being married to me.'

She stared at him, feeling suddenly as though he were a total stranger. Dear lord, surely he didn't believe that? Surely he knew she was deeply in love with him? Even if he hadn't registered what she had told him on their wedding night, it had to be obvious to him! How could he be so blind? Couldn't he see that her only concern was for his happiness, that she tried constantly to make him happy? It was ironic, really, because she knew damned well that it was he who regarded their marriage as being on trial. Hadn't he asked her, the night of his proposal, whether she would give it a go? *Give it a go—* what else could that have meant?

The awkward moment was shattered, and thereafter not mentioned again, by the arrival of two American people they had met on the beach. The couple came in full of smiles and chatter, asking if they might join Coralie and Jake. She had never felt so grateful to anyone in her life.

'But of course!' she said hastily, shifting her beach-bag to make room on the chair next to her. 'Sit near me, Cheryl, and tell me why it is that you're so much more tanned than I am—when you've only been here for ten days?'

On the evening before their departure for London, Coralie had something new to worry about. It had been six weeks since her last period and, any minute now, Jake was going to notice. They had been in Barbados for four weeks. Not for one moment did she think she might be pregnant, because she knew she could not be, she knew that her body had simply gone a bit haywire while making an adjustment. It wasn't that that worried her, it was just that she dreaded having another unpleasant scene with her husband. She did not want him questioning her, maybe accusing her of neglect, and she did not want to be in a position of having to defend herself. She was getting tired of that. It was always she who made the effort, never Jake, and she did not like this pattern that was evolving between them. She was

getting tired of pussyfooting around his sensibilities—
while he showed no concern for hers.

She was packing for both of them when he came back
from his walk that evening, slipping his arms around her
waist from behind. They'd had a splendid meal in the
hotel restaurant, and when Coralie had said she must
start on the suitcases Jake had gone off on his own.

'Leave that,' he said, his hands reaching to cup her
breasts. 'This is our last night, and right now I have
something else in mind for you.' He turned her around,
flipping the lid of the suitcase closed before he kissed
her.

Coralie melted against him as always, returning his
kiss with all the hunger he was showing for her. She could
not resist Jake physically, not that she wanted to. She
loved him and she loved making love with him. His ex-
pertise as a lover continued to lead her into new and
wonderful discoveries. Every time they made love it was
different, even more exciting than the last time. As far
as she was concerned she was still a novice, still learning
in this, a new dimension in her life.

They made love slowly that night, savouring one
another, lingering over every kiss and caress, until they
were both transported beyond the point of no return.
They slept briefly and they made love again, and on it
went until the early hours of the morning.

Coralie fell asleep with a smile on her face, unworried
that she would have to get up earlier than usual in order
to finish the packing. In those few moments at least,
nothing at all mattered to her except that she was en-
folded in Jake's arms.

CHAPTER TEN

'ENOUGH, Stuart, enough!' Jake, Coralie and her stepson were seated at the kitchen table with Mrs Everly. The newlyweds had been home for less than two hours, and they were going through the photographs they had taken on their honeymoon. Stuart was, as ever, full of questions, and Coralie was holding up her hands in defence against his bombardment. 'Question after question after question!' She laughed. 'Tell me what you've been up to, instead. Have you been a good boy for Mrs Everly?'

'That reminds me,' the housekeeper said, 'among the pile of post waiting for you is a package marked "proofs". I suppose it's the proofs of your wedding photos.'

Coralie smiled. 'Good, I'm longing to see them. But not,' she added firmly, 'tonight. I'm fit to drop right now, so I'll stay in suspense till the morning.'

Jake nodded. They were both tired after their long journey, and it was past Stuart's bedtime, too. He was still on school holidays, so it didn't matter too much; in any case, he was hyper at the moment, still excited at his parents' return.

He kept switching from one lap to another, as if he didn't know who he wanted to hug the most. At the moment it was Jake. 'Why don't you look at the photos now, Daddy?'

'Because you, young man, are going to bed and I'm going to give you your bath now.'

169

There was a lot of grumbling, but Stuart complied when his father raised an eyebrow, a look that managed to be both questioning and warning at the same time. 'Oh, all right. But I have been good, you know,' he added, turning to Coralie. 'You can ask Mrs Everly.'

'Oh, I intend to,' she said, smiling at the housekeeper. Mrs Everly was going to be sorely missed; she would be with them now only until they found a suitable replacement.

'Has he been good?' Coralie asked her when Jake had taken Stuart off to the bathroom.

'Oh, yes, he's never much trouble, as you know.'

'And what about you? How are things with you? Are you all set for your new life in Bournemouth?'

'You can say that again.' As if she thought she had been tactless, she added quickly, 'I mean—I'll miss you, of course, all of you. It isn't that——'

'I know,' Coralie smiled. 'I know what you mean. But we'll keep in touch. And we'll see you from time to time, won't we?'

'Oh, I do hope so! I'd like that. I'd like to know how Stuart is doing and...' She paused, looking at the younger woman carefully. 'And you and Mr Samuel, too. I take it everything is all right?'

'What do you mean?' Coralie asked, hoping she looked suitably nonplussed. Did it show? Was the fact that things were not as she would wish them to be detectable? If so, who was giving it away, herself or Jake? Or both?

'I suppose you're just tired from your journey,' the housekeeper answered evasively, looking again at the photographs. 'Barbados looks so beautiful, and aren't you brown? I never go brown, I just go red and it's very annoying. I used to think I'd grow out of it but I never did! Have you lost weight?' she went on, looking from a picture of a bikini-clad Coralie to the real thing. 'Or am I imagining it?'

'You're imagining it. I ate so much there, even you would have been satisfied.'

'Humph! I dread to think *what* you were eating, though.'

'Well, it wasn't roast beef and Yorkshire pudding,' Coralie conceded, laughing uproariously.

She had resolved to take life as it came, simply to let the days in her new life at home with Jake unfold, and it worked well to begin with. For almost two weeks things went quite smoothly. She and Jake interviewed prospective housekeepers together and they always agreed afterwards in their observations about the various applicants. After seeing seven people, they had still not found a suitable replacement.

'Mrs Everly will be thinking we're doing it on purpose,' Coralie said laughingly. She and Jake were just getting into bed, and she was in a particularly light frame of mind. She was not pregnant, she had discovered that afternoon. It had got to the point where she had seriously begun to wonder, where her confidence had started to wane; being thrown out of sync like that was a new experience for her and she had begun to worry. 'Do you think we should let her go in any case?' she went on. 'It doesn't seem fair to keep her hanging on here when I can cope perfectly well myself.'

'You think so?' Jake said, reaching to switch off the lamp on his side of the bed.

'Yes, we should let her go and——'

'I didn't mean that. I was asking whether you really think you can cope.'

'Oh, I see. Of course I can.' She was working on their living-room at the moment. It was a big job, but they had agreed there was no hurry, that she could go at her own pace and still give her attention to Stuart. 'I've been taking advantage of Mrs Everly's being here, I mean her being so familiar to Stuart. When we find someone new, I'll make a few changes in the running of things. As a matter of fact, I've been thinking that we don't really need someone to live in, albeit in the cottage. We could manage with daily help.'

'That's up to you,' Jake said, in a tone that made her turn to look at him.

Her lamp was still on, and she found herself looking at his profile. He seemed more interested in the ceiling than in her. What was the matter with him now? There was something bothering him, but what? Or had she imagined a sudden tightness in his voice? She sighed inwardly, and then it dawned on her. 'By the way,' she said casually, 'I'm not pregnant, Jake. I told you I wasn't.'

'I'm very glad to hear it,' he said, turning on to his side, with his back to her.

His action hurt her. Had he turned his back on her because they couldn't make love tonight—or for another reason? Either way, it hurt her. She blinked back angry tears, feeling sick and tired of the guessing game she was involved in yet again. 'Jake,' she said softly, 'please talk to me. There's something on your mind.'

For seconds he said nothing, nor did he turn to her. 'I'm dead beat, Coralie. I worked a twelve-hour day today, in case you didn't notice.'

She turned off her lamp, trying hard to suppress her anger. In case she didn't notice? Damn him, how could she not have? That was one way in which he had not changed. Or rather, he had reverted to his old ways. There had been a period in their relationship when he'd worked a normal day like any other person, but not any more. He was slipping back into his old ways of being a workaholic—and without reason. She knew he had nothing pressing professionally at the moment. That much he had told her. But he had added that he was always busy... and that she shouldn't knock it, that his being busy at work was *not* cause for complaint. But there was more to it than that, and he was just as aware of this as she was. The difference was that she was prepared to talk things through, but Jake was not.

Futilely, she tried to sleep. But how could she? The gulf between her and Jake had opened up again. It had never really closed, and the irony was that there had been no gulf at all prior to their getting married. She turned to look at him in the darkness, her eyes fixed on the outline of his body. It reminded her of their wedding night, of the way he had teased her by keeping his back to her, then. He wasn't teasing tonight, though. He wasn't even going to hold her in his arms as he went to sleep.

So be it, she thought angrily, because she was damned if she was going to make a move towards him.

As it happened, Coralie found a new housekeeper the following day, a cheerful widow in her mid-forties who had excellent references and to whom she took an immediate liking. Her name was Esther, and since Coralie did not feel particularly strongly on the matter she took her on full-time. Mrs Everly left at the end of that week and Esther moved into the cottage a couple of days later. It was admittedly handy to have a built-in babysitter, as it were, and Esther did not mind in the least when she was asked to do this.

Coralie and Jake were going to dinner at his sister's, of whom they had seen nothing since they had got back from their honeymoon, and for the first time in weeks Jake seemed to be wholly himself. He was full of fun and good humour, and the evening with Jean and Greg went beautifully.

There were a few minutes early on, before dinner, when Coralie was alone with Jean in the kitchen and Jean said laughingly that she was relieved to see things were going well between Coralie and Jake.

'Why shouldn't they?' Coralie said with practised nonchalance. 'Had you thought something was wrong between us?'

'Not I, my father.'

'Godfrey? Why? What do you mean?'

Jean looked up, she was basting meat and she turned deliberately to look straight at Coralie. 'Well, Daddy said to me, right after you and Jake had left the wedding reception, that things were not as they should be between you and Jake. He said he'd been watching you for several days, and that whatever ailed you was more than pre-wedding nerves.'

Coralie managed a laugh, a shrug, a denial. 'No, there was nothing more than pre-wedding nerves. I did have a bad case of them, though, I admit!' So she had been right, she thought, in thinking Jake's father a very shrewd old man. He had known, he had noticed, when nobody else had—before the wedding. She was beginning to wonder now, how long it would be before everybody was wondering what was wrong. It was starting to show and she knew it. But she could not have admitted it to Jean any more than Jean would press her on the point, any more than she could have asked about Jake and Alison, about the possibility that Jake was still in love with her. It had been tempting to talk, tempting to ask that particular question, but she had pushed away the temptation. She had been too scared, afraid that she might not like what she would hear.

She and Jake made love when they got home that night, that was how long his good humour lasted, until around midnight. But their lovemaking was subtly different. Coralie had the feeling that at some level he did not, in fact, want her. It was difficult to put into words, it was just that—on the one hand he seemed unable to resist her, but she felt sure he would have if he could. And she was not imagining things this time, there was no peaceful aftermath, no holding one another. Jake turned over and went straight to sleep.

The dismay that settled inside her was like a heavy stone in her heart. Determinedly she reminded herself of her resolve and tried to convince herself that things would be better the next day. For several days, that was the pattern of her life. She kept a bright and cheerful exterior, but inwardly she was weeping, knowing that things could not possibly continue as they were.

The end came on the following Sunday when she was in the second guest bedroom, painting the ceiling. Quite suddenly the door burst open, being thrown back so hard that it slammed against the wall and rocked on its hinges. Jake stood in the middle of the room and glared at Coralie, who was perched tentatively on the ladder.

'Jake! What on earth——'

'Get down here! I want words with you.'

She did not respond with anger, she responded with a dismay that almost choked her. She made her way carefully to the floor and looked at him, wondering what she had done.

'I just walked in on Stuart and found him looking at our wedding photographs,' he said, his voice shaking with fury. His eyes were like ice, staring into hers as if he were fit to kill her. 'And he looked up at me and asked me why he's never seen pictures of my wedding to his real mother, why he's never seen a picture of her at all.'

Coralie shrugged, wondering why he was angry with *her*. 'So? I told you that would happen one day.'

'Exactly!' he shouted. Then in a much louder voice, 'And I want to know whether you put him up to it.'

'What?' She actually, literally, saw red. All the breath seemed to vanish from her body and for split seconds she was dizzy, completely disorientated. Several thoughts crammed into her mind all in the same instant. She had to get out of here, out of this house, away from him. If she didn't, she would do or say something she would regret for the rest of her life. This was just like the old days, just the same as it had been at the very beginning of their relationship, almost detail for detail. She was working in a different room, that was all. She was married to the man now, that was all. God in heaven, that was *all*! Because she didn't really know him any better than she had known him then, did she? Who was he, what was he? Jake Samuel, her husband—he might just as well be the stranger he had been several months ago.

Dazedly she took one look at him and bolted towards the door.

He caught hold of her before she even reached it. 'Damn you! Answer me!'

'Get your hands off me! No, I did *not* put him up to it. I wouldn't do that to the child. How dare you?' She was shouting just as loudly as he, and Stuart was certain to hear all this. It was that realisation that finally drove her out, her fear for Stuart, his reaction to what he was hearing.

'Coralie——'

'Let go of me!' She spun round, wrenching her arm from Jake's grasp, at the same time letting fly with her other arm. She slapped him for all she was worth, screaming at him. *'Do not attribute to me your own lack of sensitivity!'*

She remained there only for the time it took to register the shock on his face. Then she was gone. She fled from the house, hoping and praying that the keys to her van were in the ignition. They were. She shoved the gears into reverse and backed the vehicle wildly off the drive. She had switched to first and was pulling away, her tyres shrieking noisily, before Jake emerged, yelling at her.

He was going to come after her, she knew it. What chance of escape did she have with a Jaguar chasing her rickety old van? None at all. It was for this reason that she swung off the road leading to the bungalow, diverting quickly down a maze of country lanes. Jake was not going to find her, he absolutely was not going to find her!

Nor did he. Two miles later there was a sudden spluttering from her vehicle, as if it were coughing in protest at her ill-treatment. Thirty seconds later it died on her and, incredulously, she realised she had run out of petrol. Stupidly she stared at the dashboard, wondering what to do next. Then the keys caught her eye and relief washed over her. Her flat. The key to her flat was on the ring with the other keys. She took them out of the ignition, locked up the van and started walking. It took no time at all for her to do something she had never done in her life—she hitched a lift into Salisbury.

CHAPTER ELEVEN

THE FLAT seemed to welcome her. Everything was exactly as she had left it. It was a sanctuary. It was her real home, it was where she really belonged. Leaving here, marrying Jake, had been a mistake. Hadn't she wondered whether she might be making the biggest mistake of her life? Well, she had.

She flung herself across the settee and burst into tears. She sobbed for a long time, how long she had no idea. She allowed herself to cry and cry, realising as she did so how much she had been holding back for many weeks. The floodgates continued to open; it was as if with each new thought, each scene remembered, another well of tears was ready to come forth.

When the tears finally began to subside she found herself shuddering in their aftermath, making little gasping sounds as her breathing steadied. She felt better, much better. She reached for a cushion and lay down to sleep, a dreamless sleep.

Somewhere a bell began to ring, a shrill, disturbing noise. Coralie surfaced long enough to realise it was the telephone. She dragged herself from the settee and unplugged it, knowing a sense of satisfaction which was almost childish. If it were Jake ringing, he could go to hell. Of course it was Jake. Nobody else would think to ring her here.

The next time she opened her eyes it was twilight. She got up and closed the curtains, remembering with gratitude that Sophie had gone away on holiday. There would be no disturbances. She could stay here where she was safe, where there were no hurts, where she could begin to heal. But what was she going to do? What on earth was she going to do?

She made some coffee. It was as far ahead as she was capable of thinking.

When her doorbell rang, her eyes flew to the clock. Irrelevantly she thought how faithfully it had been ticking away the hours, the days, the weeks since she had married Jake. At some level she acknowledged that her crazy thoughts were a deliberate distraction from what was happening. The doorbell was ringing and it was Jake. It was Jake and he was not going to go away. He knew she was in here.

As if to confirm it, his voice came booming through the door. 'Open up! Dammit, Coralie, open this door before I smash it to pieces!'

It was curious how his anger affected her. She felt no reciprocal emotion this time, she knew only a sudden stillness inside. Calmly she got up to let him in, knowing not only that this confrontation was inevitable but also that she could cope with it, would cope with it, precisely as she wished to. There would be no more shouting from her, she would tell him simply that their marriage was over, that it had been a sham from the beginning.

That was how she greeted him. She looked up at him and stepped aside, allowing him to pass. When he reached the living-room, she said, 'It's over, Jake. We'll start divorce proceedings as quickly as possible. Marrying you was a monumental mistake.'

For seconds he just looked at her, giving her the impression that these were the last words he had expected to hear. Then he seemed to subside physically: his shoulders hunched, his head bowed in a an attitude of defeat. He nodded. 'If that's what you want.'

On hearing that, Coralie's inner stillness suddenly vanished. The room seemed to shift before her eyes, so swift was the change of emotion in her. Without re-alising it she was shouting again, angrier than she had ever been in her life. 'If that's what I want? If that's what *I* want? Of course it isn't what I want. Damn you, Jake, it's what *you* want.'

'No...'

'Yes. I've got the message. I got it weeks ago. But that just goes to show what a fool I am. I love you so much that I turned a blind eye to it. The writing was on the wall the very day we got married—but I ignored it.'

'What,' he asked incredulously, 'in God's name are you talking about? The writing was on the wall?' His voice rose, it had begun as a whisper but it was rising now on every word. 'And who put it there? Not I! I've done everything in my power——' Abruptly he stopped. He turned away from her, shaking his head. When next he spoke he was whispering again...and she knew he was near to tears. 'No, that's not true. I—tried to do all I could to make you happy, but instead I've driven you away, haven't I?'

Coralie steeled herself. She was standing perfectly still, just a few feet from him, and she closed her eyes against what was happening, against the emotions he was stirring in her. Never before had she seen Jake like this, close to tears if not actually crying, and she did not want to go on with him, with this. She did not want to be weak and let him get to her. It was too late, anyway; there was no point in any of this. For too long she had made an effort to behave naturally with him—but it had all been false, it had been nothing but a repression, a repression of her emotions. Well, she was tired of not being herself, she was tired of having to watch her every word, she was sick and tired of having to *act*.

'Yes,' she said baldly. 'You have driven me away.'

Whether he really didn't hear her or whether he affected not to hear her, she didn't know. He turned to look at her, carrying on where he had left off. 'The funny thing is—and this is going to sound perverse to you—I knew I was doing it. I knew I was closing off from you and I couldn't seem to stop myself.'

Unconsciously, she crossed her arms when he looked at her, a gesture of self-defence which spoke for itself.

'Coralie, please,' he went on, 'please forgive me.'

No! Her mind screamed the word, her arms moving downwards to hug her midriff. 'It's no good, Jake. Get out of here; I'm not prepared to talk to you. I've tried and tried to do that, and it's too late now.'

'I know,' he said quietly. 'I know you've tried, but I was...too stupid, or too proud, to respond.'

As he took a step towards her, she moved backwards. 'No, Jake. Don't touch me. I meant what I said, it's over.'

'Don't say that, Coralie. I'm aware of what I've been doing, at times I seemed almost to be outside myself, watching my own behaviour. Watching and wishing that I could stop being a fool, that I could confide in you, tell you how afraid I felt—about us. I don't lack sensitivity, you were wrong about that. I think I've got too much, more than is good for me. I've been afraid all along, but all I did was make things worse. God in heaven, do you know how frightened I've been these past few hours?'

'What? What do you mean?' He had been afraid all along? A trickle of understanding filtered through to her, but she had to know more, she had to make him talk.

He misunderstood her question, he thought she was asking about his fears of today. 'I mean I've been searching for you, I've been going out of my mind. I drove straight here to begin with, taking it for granted you'd have fled here. Then I went home to see if you'd gone back there. Nothing. Stuart was with me and——'

'Stuart? Oh, Jake!'

'He's all right, he's more than all right. He's with Esther now, she came home at five. I—anyhow, I went searching for you then and I found your van, abandoned. Can you imagine what went through my mind? I had no idea where to begin—you might have been anywhere. You might have been picked up on the road and murdered. Anything. I went back to the bungalow eventually and started ringing you here.'

'I unplugged the telephone.'

'So I've noticed.' He smiled, seemingly in spite of himself. 'Oh, Coralie——'

He caught hold of her and she stiffened in his arms; she did so deliberately because she had to push him, she had to get at the truth, she had to understand him fully once and for all. 'No, Jake. It's over, I told you——'

'It'll never be over between us.'

'That's nonsense, I've——'

'Never,' he said. 'Because you love me. You really do love me, I'm sure of it now.'

Swiftly her head came up. 'What do you mean by that?'

'I mean I didn't believe it when you first said it, I put it down to the...madness of the moment. Let's face it, you were hardly thinking straight at the time!'

She would not have believed herself capable of blushing in front of Jake again, not these days, not after they had shared the most exquisite intimacy. But blush she did, much to his delight. He pulled her tightly against him and brought his mouth down on hers, kissing her wildly, kissing her as if that, rather than words, would convey all he wanted her to know. He was like that, he was an extremely passionate man physically, but she realised now that he used this to cover for a lack in him, a lack he was well aware of.

'And you?' she said at length, her eyes challenging. 'What exactly do you feel for me, Jake?'

'Don't be silly, you know what I feel for you. I've just shown you.'

She smiled inwardly. Yes, she did know, finally, what he felt for her. 'Supposing you tell me, supposing you put it into words?'

'I'm——' He looked away, he didn't let go of her but he looked down at the floor. 'I was never much good at that sort of thing, you must know that.'

'Just tell me, Jake. It can't be that difficult. Why were you so worried when you thought I'd gone missing?'

There was pain in his eyes when he brought them back to hers. 'I thought I'd lost you. I mean, lost you for ever...'

And then she understood fully. With a small cry, she flung herself against him and hugged him desperately. Oh, God, how wrong she had been! How stupid! He loved her, all right—why had she never realised it? Why had it been so important that he should tell her? Why had she let her happiness hinge on hearing the actual words? Hadn't he shown it in lots of little ways, just as he did with Stuart? It was true—to be fair it *was* true, Jake was not much good at this sort of thing, he never had been.

She thought back to their wedding day; she thought about all the care he had taken to make it perfect, the infinite patience he had shown with her that night, how he had helped her over her nervousness. It had been that nervousness, combined with the certain knowledge that he did not love her, that had made her behave all wrongly on that day. From then on it had got worse—and much of it was her fault. This flat, for instance, her reluctance to let go of it must have made Jake feel as insecure as she had.

'Jake, something awful has been going on between us, and we're both responsible. I wonder if you realise how insidious it's been? I've only just realised how much you feel for me. I've only just realised,' she added bravely, looking straight at him, 'that you love me. I believed you didn't. Right up until a few minutes ago, I believed you didn't. That was why I remained reluctant to give up this flat, which was a terrible mistake. I never stopped to think of the effect that would have on you.'

'I hated it,' he admitted. 'I told you in Barbados, I thought you regarded our marriage as nothing more than an experiment.'

'I know. But I'd got to the stage where I was convinced you were still in love with Alison. I thought you were still hung up about her death, to the point where it was affecting your relationship with me as it used to affect your relationship with Stuart.'

'I—wait a minute.' He stepped away from her, looking weary, and crossed to sit in the armchair by the fire.

'You were right about that. I mean, in a way you were right.'

Coralie let out a long and ragged sigh. Wordlessly, she nodded. She had realised this minutes ago, when she had asked herself why he was so angry—why, if he didn't love her, he could react to the past several hours the way he had. Jake had loved her all along, he'd just never been able to say it. And in the belief that she didn't love him, he had become afraid of losing her—as he had lost his first wife. Perversely, as he'd put it, he had made matters worse by closing off from her, by being too proud to tell her all this.

Happily, he was able to tell her now. 'Losing Alison was—well, I'm sure you can understand what it did to me, what a shock it was. I've loved you for a long time, Coralie.' He looked at her proudly, as if he'd broken through a barrier by putting it into words. 'But,' he went on, 'I was afraid, afraid of allowing myself to feel my love for you, just as I was afraid to allow myself to feel my love for Stuart. The fear of suffering again the pain I went through when Alison died was just too strong. I couldn't face it.'

She smiled gently in acknowledgement and understanding. 'And I didn't tell you how I felt until after we'd tied the knot. And then you didn't believe me, so you've been anticipating the day when I would walk out on you, and that would be just as bad as if I died—— Oh, *Jake*! Is this why you've been so fanatical about me taking the Pill?'

He looked at her helplessly, nodding. 'I told you I've been stupid. But at least I've realised that denying yourself joy for fear that it might one day stop is just that—stupid.'

Coralie ran to him; she threw herself on to his lap and held him tightly. 'Then you just listen to me, Jacob Samuel, and listen well. When and if I have a baby, I am not going to die in the process. Do you understand?'

She could feel him nodding again, his lips against her temple. 'I know. I know you won't. Oh, Coralie, I do love you.' He whispered the words against her hair, holding her against him as if she were precious. 'Thank God I lost my temper today, thank God I stormed in and accused you like that!'

The wedding photos. Stuart. She smiled. Anything could have precipitated this, she and Jake had been sitting on a time-bomb for weeks. 'Forget that. Just tell me how you're going to handle it—with Stuart, I mean.'

'I already have. I dug out my old photograph albums before I left to come here. I wanted to be able to tell you I'd done that.'

'And how did your son react, Jake?'

'With happy interest, not a hint of tears or anything.'

Coralie lifted her head for a kiss. 'Well done,' she said at length.

He smiled. 'I love you. Hey, it gets easier the more I say it!'

'Then keep saying it,' she laughed. 'Don't ever stop communicating with me again. Keep on saying it, Jake. Tell me every day for the rest of my life.'

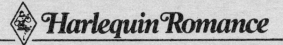

Harlequin Romance

Coming Next Month

#3007   BLUEPRINT FOR LOVE   Amanda Clark
Shannon West knows that renovating an old house means uncovering its hidden strengths. When she meets Griff Marek, an embittered architect—and former sports celebrity—she learns that love can do the same thing.

#3008   HEART OF MARBLE   Helena Dawson
Cressida knows it's risky taking a job sight unseen, but Sir Piers Aylward's offer to help him open Clarewood Priory to the public is too good to miss. Then she discovers that he wants nothing to do with the planning—or with her.

#3009   TENDER OFFER   Peggy Nicholson
Did Clay McCann really think he could cut a path through Manhattan, seize her father's corporation—and her—without a fight? Apparently he did! And Rikki wondered what had happened to the Clay she'd idolized in her teens.

#3010   NO PLACE LIKE HOME   Leigh Michaels
Just when Kaye's dreams are within reach—she's engaged to a kind, gentle man who's wealthy enough to offer real security—happy-go-lucky Brendan McKenna shows up, insisting that *he's* the only man who can really bring her dreams to life....

#3011   TO STAY FOREVER   Jessica Steele
Kendra travels to Greece without hesitation to answer her cousin Faye's call for help. And Eugene, Faye's husband, seems grateful. Not so his associate, Damon Niarkos, the most hateful man Kendra's ever met. What right does he have to interfere?

#3012   RISE OF AN EAGLE   Margaret Way
Morgan's grandfather Edward Hartland had always encouraged the enmity between her and Tyson—yet in his will he divided the Hartland empire between them. Enraged, Morgan tries to convince Ty that he's a usurper in her home!

Available in October wherever paperback books are sold, or through Harlequin Reader Service:

In the U.S.
901 Fuhrmann Blvd.
P.O. Box 1397
Buffalo, N.Y. 14240-1397

In Canada
P.O. Box 603
Fort Erie, Ontario
L2A 5X3

® **Harlequin American Romance**®

SUMMER.

The sun, the surf, the sand . . .

One relaxing month by the sea was all Zoe, Diana and Gracie ever expected from their four-week stays at Gull Cottage, the luxurious East Hampton mansion. They never thought they'd soon be sharing those long summer days—or hot summer nights—with a special man. They never thought that what they found at the beach would change their lives forever. But as Boris, Gull Cottage's resident mynah bird said: "Beware of summer romances. . . ."

Join Zoe, Diana and Gracie for the summer of their lives. Don't miss the GULL COTTAGE trilogy in American Romance: #301 *Charmed Circle* by Robin Francis (July 1989), #305 *Mother Knows Best* by Barbara Bretton (August 1989) and #309 *Saving Grace* by Anne McAllister (September 1989).

GULL COTTAGE—because a month can be the start of forever . . .

Harlequin Regency Romance™

Romance the way it was *always* meant to be!

The time is 1811, when a Regent Prince rules the empire. The place is London, the glittering capital where rakish dukes and dazzling debutantes scheme and flirt in a dangerously exciting game. Where marriage is the passport to wealth and power, yet every girl hopes secretly for love....

Welcome to Harlequin Regency Romance where reading is an adventure and romance is *not* just a thing of the past! Two delightful books a month.

Available wherever Harlequin Books are sold.

Harlequin Historicals

Step into a world of pulsing adventure, gripping emotion and lush sensuality with these evocative love stories penned by today's best-selling authors in the highest romantic tradition. Pursuing their passionate dreams against a backdrop of the past's most colorful and dramatic moments, our vibrant heroines and dashing heroes will make history come alive for you.

Watch for two new Harlequin Historicals each month, available wherever Harlequin books are sold. History was never so much fun—you won't want to miss a single moment!

GHIST-1